VOICES

OF THE

VOID

By
David V. Stewart

Voices of the Void

Andrew walked down the gallery, watching the slowly bobbing reflection on the waxed floor from the bright artificial windows to his left. Looking out as he entered the wide, clean foyer, it was hard to believe he had just stepped through a grit-caked airlock that opened into darkness. Comfortable furniture lined the walls in bright colors, upholstered in a synthetic material made to look like weaved cotton. The rubber-soled boots of his EV suit even squeaked as he walked; the dust collection system was still working at full capacity. The automated maintenance system was top-of-the-line; it would be years before it needed its own round of repairs, and the reactor that powered the colony would likely take centuries to die. Andrew reminded himself of this as he looked at the details of human life around him.

This section was the school. A book sat on a nearby work table, closed and abandoned, ignored by the robots and machines that cleaned the room... Andrew couldn't guess how many times they had passed it over. On a nearby bulletin board, there were pinned a variety of drawings depicting scenes that were more-or-less earth-like: children playing on grass under a yellow sun, rain and rainbows, castles and cars on busy streets. Odd, considering that it was likely none of the children had ever seen Earth, any other garden planet, or even a bright yellow sun for that matter. Andrew paused and looked around himself, and thought it likely none of them ever would. But there was a chance, or else he wouldn't be here. He spied on one of the nearby desks another drawing, and his eye became fixed on it.

He walked toward it, looking down at the floor of artificial maple, each section printed to be as unique as real wood, and saw a black scuff mark that had stood up to the passage of the cleaning machines.

Andrew looked up and felt suddenly queasy.

The large room was full of children of all ages, sitting on the neat couches or working at tables. From a distant hall, a teenage boy careened toward him on old-fashioned rolling skates. A young woman – a teacher, by her professional dress, stood at the entrance to a nearby classroom, her arms crossed seriously, though she smiled slightly as she watched the youth. Her light brown hair blew around her shoulders as the boy passed her. Another teacher – a middle-aged man – slipped behind another door, pretending not to notice the boy.

The young teacher called to the teenage boy, "Astin!" and though he knew she was looking to the rebellious youth, Andrew could have sworn the teacher caught his eye. "Astin what do you think you are doing?!"

She's pretty. The thought careened into his consciousness unbidden, though not as unwelcome as other sentiments that intruded so. Andrew could suddenly see the details in her eyes, as if he were looking into them just centimeters away. They were blue, and reflected the artificial day of a skylight above in a bright white halo.

The image disappeared as Andrew came back into himself. He flinched as the boy on skates tried to stop in front of him, but tripped, scuffing the floor with the rubber brake on his skates, falling onto his side and sliding away, grunting softly. He slid into, or rather, *through,* Andrew.

And then the vision faded. The sounds of playing children turned to hallow reverberation, and the beautiful teacher turned translucent as she stepped toward him, intent on helping the fallen teenager. Then she was gone.

"Damnit," Andrew said to himself, forcing the word out of his mouth. His visor was fogging up with his rapid breath. He checked the computer on his wrist and, seeing that the air was clean and clear, he pressed the release button at his neck. His helmet and visor split into tiny ribbons, then disappeared into his collar. He breathed deeply.

"Damn fool, getting distracted like that," he said aloud to himself. With the helmet removed, he was suddenly aware of the reverb of his voice in the empty room and the soft clicking of a fan's bearing somewhere in the ventilation system. The wonder of the vision was quickly replaced with his usual sense of unease. He looked down and checked the receiver of his rifle – an antique weapon, but one that he knew functioned better within atmospheres than his plasma gun, which he kept slung on his back. It was toggled over to *auto*. Andrew shook his head and toggled it back to safe, distrusting his instincts.

He stepped toward the picture on the desk, hoping to provoke another vision (which he had, ironically, intended to avoid by staring at the faux-wood floor), and hoping also that if he were to slip back to the past, he could, with his wits more about him, actually look for his quarry. He let his rifle hang and picked up the picture. It was of a castle, colored with grey pencil and highly detailed, but there were little modern colony buildings instead of a medieval village surrounding it.

Probably better if I don't slip back, he said inside himself. *I need to find her in the present. A past vision does nothing.* A void echoed back, and Andrew sighed.

Andrew looked to the manila door from which he had seen the young teacher emerge. It was shut. He could see through a small window a few empty desks. He felt a strong compulsion to open the door and look around, provoke another vision.

She's likely dead, his voice said to himself. He knew the voice – part of his fractured self – was right. They had played too long at that once already. Andrew nodded his head.

He couldn't control the power, at least not yet, but he was beginning to understand what would cause it to present itself. Perhaps in the future, he would be able to look back in time at will, not be thrust into it at the behest of some echo in his brain and lose all sense of what "the present" meant. Perhaps… but such experiments would have to wait.

Andrew put the picture back down and stepped away from the desk. He walked through the open school toward where his readout said the primary elevators were. This sector had to be empty. He walked down a long and narrow hallway, the rustle of his suit and his soft steps the only sound.

When he reached the elevators, he noticed the doorway to the dormitory overflows was open. The lights were shining brightly all the way down a long, straight hallway. He could only see the first few doors, and they were all shut.

Andrew looked back at the slick steel doors of the closest elevator. A glowing panel above indicated that the car was paused on the sixth level. He tried to remember how deep things went, information he gathered while pouring over the technical details of the plant during his trip to the planet, but his memory felt hard to access.

"Probably goes pretty deep, but not from the dorms, yeah?" he said aloud, listening to his voice die in the artificial, fabric-lined corridor. He slipped his right glove off to operate the computer panel and call up the elevator. After hurriedly going through the motions, he brought his rifle around and touched the trigger, feeling the familiar steel against his fingertip. He let the weapon fall back into its bungee sling and tucked his glove into the belt of his suit.

The lift moved slowly, and Andrew could hear the sliding and grinding of the pulleys above, shaking off old, dry dust. He glanced over at the dormitory again. He stepped toward it, seeing more of the plain blue doors appear around shallow recesses in the hallway.

"Hello?" he called loudly. "I'm here from…" He paused and thought about his employer. His mission from Saul Toro was not officially from the Iber Colony Counsel. "I'm here to help. Is there anyone out there?" He brought his rifle back up and shouldered it, intending to fire a shot, but then thought better of it. "Anyone alive?"

The elevator doors opened, and he glanced at an empty and pristine car. He turned from it and stepped toward the dormitory hallway. A tall computer panel stood next to the open blast doors. Andrew saw that it could be used to page the rooms, but also saw, since this was an overflow dormitory, that only certain rooms could be paged. He could go through the list, one by one, and make sure there was nobody simply hiding from him.

"What would they be hiding from?"

Part of his mind answered to him, almost against his will. A single word – a *concept* – from a sector of himself he had, for reasons of sanity, maintained little contact with.

Wr't'lra'a The word drew itself out, all guttural nonsense, but in the image remained. *Wrtla,* a voice inside said back.

Could it be? He thought. *Could there really be more of them?* The situation seemed to fit, but then again there were many things in the universe that could swallow a colony of humans whole. *But leave everything so perfect? No! They walked away. They walked down. To it.*

The sliver of his former self that had surged forward seemed to cry wordlessly after its interjection, demanding to become one with the other pieces of Andrew's mind. The self he was before – his memories, his identity – had something more to say, but it had been touched too deeply by the ancient unknowable void. The hunter he had created out of the shards of that contact asserted itself and shut the old, broken Andrew away. His old consciousness was now an echo – useful if needed, but safely locked up.

Andrew took a quick picture of the room list with his computer and stepped into the dormitory hallway. It was carpeted and clean. He brought up the list on the screen attached to his left forearm. Normally he would use the heads-up display on his helmet, but he had removed it to breathe the air of the place.

"J-115," he said aloud. A sliver of his mind touched his consciousness, and he felt a pang of dread again. He frowned and focused as he walked to the first occupied dormitory, bringing his rifle forward in its sling just in case. He found the door unlocked, and it pushed in with a slight squeak of the hinges. Automatic lights flickered on, revealing a Spartan flat.

"Anyone home?"

As he expected, silence was all that greeted him.

He stepped in and looked around briefly. In the bathroom a toothbrush sat perched on a deep sink. A personal computer sat on a table near the made bed, dead and unplugged.

Andrew took a breath and listened to his own thoughts.

It would take a long time to check every room. The dread returned, and tapping on the edge of his current consciousness was an idea he didn't want to consider. It tapped again, and he groaned, wondering if it were prescience or just his imagination.

He stepped out of the empty flat and continued down the hall.

"I'm checking each one, so you might as well come out if you haven't. I'm not here to hurt you."

The whir of a fan in a vent was all that responded. Then there was a sudden click, and Andrew brought up his rifle, quickly clicking off the safety. A few paces in front of him, a small door in the wall opened up, and a cleaning robot emerged. It began its daily chore, turning and running along the edge of the hallway, sucking up the dust that had collected in the last day.

Andrew chuckled and stepped forward, then was assaulted by a vision and a ringing in his ears. He reached to the wall to steady himself, but the wall wasn't there.

He was suddenly inside a large flat, stepping toward a partly open door. A smell was stuck in his nostrils like dried mud. It was a rotten smell, and he knew what made it. He pushed the door wider, looking only down the sights of his rifle, knowing that it would not save him from the horror. The lights flickered on, and his mind was fracturing further, seeing further, as if the vision could not be contained within a single moment.

He screamed as he saw a crib; the scream did not stop him from continuing forward and seeing what remained inside the simple wooden bed. Nausea scraped across the back of his head, his neck, his ears, down his throat. He could smell his own bile. He screamed with every piece of himself, screamed and bled and cried and collapsed.

Then he was standing back in the hall. The cleaner had moved one door down. His prescient self was still screaming, and though the images remained, preserved like endlessly looped video files, the screams began to slowly fade, responding to the subtle push he gave to that part of his mind. Soon it was a dull roar in his mind: echoing, distant, and yet not gone.

"No reason to continue," he said, his voice dry like reeds. "They walked away. Those that *could* walk away."

He turned away from the hall and ran back toward the elevators. As he did, the screaming finally stopped. The vision of the dead, forgotten child, seared into his retinas, burned into his memory forever, suddenly waned and began to disappear. By the time he reached the lift, the images had nearly evaporated, becoming a dream after waking, or a half-memory of a blurry photograph.

He knew what he had seen, though. His future self had seen it, and by warning him, had destroyed the vision in a paradox created by his change of course.

He stepped into the elevator. He ran his hand through the menus on the computer to run the car down to the industrial center, which was level six. *The last place this elevator went.* From there, he would test the fears and desires of his former mind. Already that part was raving, calling to him. The doors closed. Andrew kneeled and began preparing himself. He checked every magazine and battery he had. He tested the light on his front rail and affixed a bayonet to his front lug. He checked his plasma gun and made sure it was slung right where he would want it.

Lastly, he reached in his pocket and felt for the grenade he had rigged up specially to explode immediately upon setting the fuse. He would not feed the old Andrew to a *Wrtla*, whatever might happen. The finality of that decision gave him courage. He knew not whether there was a journey beyond his life through limbo or purgatory, but wherever he might go, he would go as himself.

Taking a breath, he checked his wrist computer. His vision blurred and focused. It was 10:00 hours. He tapped the computer, sure something was wrong. Perhaps it had reset the time when he had entered the mining facility, syncing with the central chronometer. Toro *had* given him the codes.

"It can't have been three hours already," he said, reassuring himself. Visions, especially those of the future, were always instantaneous.

He toggled the safety of his rifle, finding it on semi and feeling disconcerted by the fact until he remembered that he had meant to fire a warning shot down the hall.

"I'm getting out of practice," he said to himself.

The elevator slowed and the lift doors opened. He stepped out and looked down several wandering hallways which led to the lowest level of housing. Like the top floor, there was an open foyer near the elevators, but this one was clearly designed with an industrial purpose in mind. Desks and computer terminals lined every wall. Like the first floor, these were left in a state of mid-use. Some monitors still showed open documents, the image of words and draft lines burned forever into the machine, which carried on refreshing the same still image week after week. Caged doors opened off the main hall into equipment rooms and other repositories like lockers and materials storage.

A few wide sapphire windows were set in the walls, gazing out into an abyss that once was likely the well-lit beginning of the mine. The darkness beyond irritated a part of Andrew, but he resisted the urge to shine a light out one of those windows and see the rock for himself.

Andrew walked past all this, shining his light into dark corners, following his map to the next set of lifts, which would take him down into the mining area. Once again, there was no life other than the artificial buzzing of machines engaged in their daily maintenance tasks. He skipped the dormitories, knowing that if they were not empty, they would contain things he did not wish to see.

He paused as he passed a workstation, noting that a half-eaten donut remained by the keyboard, nearly desiccated. He wondered why no pest had wandered by to claim it, but then he remembered the planet's desolate surface. There would be no unwanted life in the colony, save for the microbes that came along with the colonists themselves, and he had already seen those at work on the corpse-

"Of the baby," he said aloud, and shivered. The image was dim, nearly gone, but he could imagine the horror well enough.

He paused as he turned away, noticing a few pieces of rubbish in the workstation's wastebasket. He looked around and saw, as he expected, no trash in any other basket. The robots responsible for waste management were working well, except for this one. This one contained a number of food wrappers and grease-stained napkins that the robots for some reason could not detect.

I guess the systems aren't so autonomous after all, he thought. He walked on into a wide hallway, brightly lit and floored with a composite pebble. The walls were smooth and sound absorbent. He held his rifle aloft as he rounded a bend, then found the next set of lifts. He checked every corner as he approached, his sense of foreboding growing strong again – telling him that he faced danger, and also that he was on the right track.

The lift cars that serviced the mine were, as Andrew expected, both away deep in the various digs. He looked out a nearby window. Like the others on the bottom level, it was one of few in the facility that was not made to artificially create a sense of sunlight on a garden planet. He could see running lights going down a long series of rails and cables. The lifts would slide along these, going diagonally into the mining area. In a few places, the lights were flickering or dead, and Andrew knew he had come to the end of the well-designed automated habitat created for the human miners.

He took a look at the computer panel by the lifts and noted where the cars were. One was on sector four, the other past it on sector five, which he assumed was deeper in the infinite rock of the well-named planet Gibraltar. He thought it curious that the lift cars were not on the same level, but then remembered he was operating on a set of assumptions that were, in all likelihood, bunk. It was his precognitive side's worrying about his original mind – that "Old Andrew" he kept contained and away from consciousness – that was leading him to believe in a... whatever you could call it. A demon?

"Then what are they doing in the mine, eh?" he said to himself. He called up the car from sector 4, thinking he would check there before proceeding further in. Once again he had a tickle, but this time it was a mixture of feelings. Dread still hung in the future, but there was also something else, like a quiet anticipation. He wondered which part of him felt that, and as he rolled between his minds, he was reminded of his "old" self – was there something in there calling out?

He watched the lift car approach, hanging from a steel rail, arriving much sooner than Andrew anticipated. Had it really come so far in just a few minutes? He worked against an urge to check his computer, which he knew was not functioning properly, to confirm the time.

The car moved past the windows and arrived at the steel double doors. After a few seconds of buzzing, the car opened. It was empty. Of the four lights in the ceiling, three remained lit. Andrew stepped in and told the computer to head to sector four. The motor overhead jumped to life, the doors closed, and the car lurched, heading out and down.

Through two small windows in the doors, Andrew watched the colony's headquarters shrink, cut into living rock and lined with multiple stories of lit, empty windows. Below the car was a black abyss spanned by steel and old scaffolds – the first mining site of the colony, now abandoned and depleted. Eventually, the lights shrank to dots, and he turned to the windows on the opposite side. He was hovering in the dark, the running lights on the track the only thing to remind him he was moving forward. Seconds passed, then long minutes.

The track turned and slowed. The descent leveled off as he approached sector one. It was black save for a few scattered lights. Nothing moved except for some clouds of dust as the car moved past the open landing cut into the rock and back into the dark caves. It began to get colder, and Andrew clenched his ungloved right hand. As the car rolled on, the running lights on the track growing brighter (they were newer, he reckoned), he reeled at the amount of atmosphere the colonists had created for their operation. The planet's surface was still thin and made mostly of greenhouse gases, a necessary step for even the accelerated process of creating a garden world, but the vast catacombs of the Gibraltar mine were full of fresh oxy. The way forward was wide, but always around the car earth-like air rushed like wind.

The car approached sector two. The rock ceiling came into view as the car slowed and paused at what looked like an equipment bay. A few hanging sodium lamps lit a long open avenue, lined with lockers and abandoned tools. A few computer terminals were still lit, ticking away with whatever tasks they had. The doors opened automatically. Andrew flinched and shouldered his rifle, but relaxed as a small robot rolling on tracks appeared from around a rock formation. The light on the end of its single appendage searched back and forth over the smooth floor.

"Hello!" Andrew yelled. Nothing answered him past the glow of the lamps, but the robot, not slowing, turned its light upon him.

"Greetings," it said in a warm, feminine voice as it approached. "Sector two is not staffed today. Are you looking for someone?"

Andrew felt a bead of sweat pop on his brow, despite the still and cold air of the bay. "Um... I might be," he said, shrugging, though he knew the robot would likely not recognize the gesture.

"Are you heading further down?" it said pleasantly, pausing in front of the open doors. "Perhaps I could share a ride with you if you are. If not, or if you do not wish to ride with me, I will wait for the next car."

"Um..." Andrew stepped away from the robot to appraise it. It took the gesture as consent and rolled into the lift. The doors closed, and the car began to move down again, the computer being operated remotely by the robot.

"Are you new?" the robot said.

"I am," Andrew said. "How did you know?"

"I haven't seen you before." Its arm and its strange light (which had dimmed to a pale blue) swiveled to regard Andrew.

"Oh," Andrew said.

"What is your name?"

Andrew thought a moment. "Toro."

"My name is Lucille. Are you married or single?"

Andrew frowned at the thing. "What is your function, if you don't mind me asking?"

"My function is autonomous maintenance of electronics and basic structures within the mining hazard zone. What is your job, Toro?"

"Why are you asking if I'm married?"

The robot dimmed its front light. "I don't have any records of you. I thought I would update the personnel files for Tracy with the identity of your spouse and children, if applicable. I know she would appreciate having it done for her."

Andrew nervously checked the safety of his rifle. He had flipped back to *auto* at some point. He put his thumb on it and slowly clicked it back twice to safe. "I'll talk to Tracy myself."

"What is your job, Toro?"

"Mining."

"I'm sorry, Toro, I meant to say-" The robot paused and clicked a few times, "What is the title of your job position?"

"Why do you want to know? I told you I'd talk to Tracy."

"What is the title of your job position?"

Andrew looked out the window. They were passing through a narrower stone passage, not hanging over an abyss any longer. It was still cold and dark. The stone had a mottled color, grey and black, with veins of iron that had not yet gone to rust in the newly oxygenated mine.

"Have you forgotten your job title?" The robot said.

"Yes," Andrew said.

"Open positions were for maintenance supervisor and demolitions technician. Does either of those sound correct?"

"Yes. Maintenance supervisor."

"Pleased to meet you, Maintenance Supervisor Toro. I am Lucille, one of the autonomous maintenance robots that operate in the mining hazard zone," it said, seemingly oblivious to its own conversation history.

"How many more of you are there?"

"Three."

"Where are they?"

"The other maintenance robots are powered down, sir."

"Why?"

"Their services have not been required."

"Why are *your* services required?"

"Sectors three and four have not been serviced in 45 days."

"Why?"

"Transport has not stopped at my service terminal in 46 days."

"*Why?*"

"I am not authorized to operate lift cars except in the presence of staff, for logistic and security reasons."

"I meant why hasn't there been any elevator stopping at your last location?"

The robot clicked. "I don't know that, sorry."

"You stopped my car. I wasn't stopping at your last location."

After a few seconds, the robot said, "I am not authorized to stop a lift car."

Andrew growled to himself softly. "You know what, Lucille, I forgot – I *am* looking for someone."

"Who are you looking for?"

"Vivian Toro."

The robot clicked. The computer terminal moved through some menus on its own. "Sorry, the network is slow."

"No worries."

The robot clicked a few more times. "Vivian is in the third grade. You can find her in the education center, either in the common area, or as a pupil of Elena Garcia."

"Thanks. I've already been to the school, and she wasn't there."

"I'm sorry I couldn't help you. You can contact the education center to see if she was out of class due to health concerns."

"I don't think it was that."

"I'm sorry; I don't have information on that."

"It's fine, Lucille."

"Thanks, Toro."

The car approached sector three. The elevator bay opened to a much smaller space. The lift stopped and the doors opened. Lucille the robot moved out into a dirty corridor, kicking up a few dust clouds to dance under the bright LEDs and warm sodium lamps which were attached to wires running along the high ceiling.

"Is this your arrival point, Supervisor Toro?" it said, pausing and *looking* back with its light.

"No. Say, Lucille..."

"What is it, Toro?"

Andrew took a slow breath, wondering if he should be so direct with a machine that could report to the unsecured network. "Do you know what happened to everyone? Where the colonists went?"

"I do not know what happened to everyone. Which colonists were you looking for?"

"All of them. They're all gone from the residential area."

"I'm sorry, but I can't seem to parse your request. Can you be more specific?"

Andrew chewed his cheek. He didn't feel quite right talking to a robot in this way, but the thing seemed harmless enough.

"Have a nice day-"

Andrew's mind shifted for a few moments, inducing nausea instantly, and then suddenly the robot was looking away. More lights were on, and brighter. A few men stood around, talking. One of them was holding a toolbox, which he put down.

"The network is fine, here," he said.

The other man took off a hard hat and scratched his bald head. "Well, it must be further down. Check out sector four."

"Maybe the demo team is playing a prank on us," the first man said.

"Not my kind of prank."

"Can we have them relay back through the robots?"

"I would think so, but the robots don't seem able to manage it on their own."

"Maybe Johnny could write a few routines for that. Seems like a good redundancy."

The other man put his hard hat back on. "Truthfully I never considered this sort of malfunction. I'll get down to sector five and check it out myself. I'm not looking forward to telling Esquivel how I lost a half-day of work, though."

The first man shrugged and picked up his toolbox, then started walking toward Andrew. He faded away, and the lights dimmed.

Lucille remained where she was, but was clicking and turning away. The lift doors began to close.

"Wait!" Andrew said, putting out a hand to stop the doors. He glanced at his computer. "I'm looking for the senior plant manager. Um…" He flipped through a few messages. "Ralph Esquivel."

Lucille turned back and dimmed its light. "He is listed as absent to work. I lack the capacity to be more specific. Shall I page him?"

"No, don't bother."

"Alright, Toro. Have a nice day."

Andrew watched the robot begin moving again. "You too, Lucille."

The doors closed, and jets of air began moving about the robot, kicking up dust and blowing it to the edges of the room. The lift started moving again, resuming its journey down into the rock at a steep incline.

Once again the walls opened up and the car slid out into icy blackness, bouncing slightly; apparently, the rails in the final sectors were not as robust here, with the supports from the ceiling or rocks below more spread out, or perhaps as a whole, it was built to a lower specification. The car swayed as it moved, but the engine above showed no signs of struggle. Andrew popped his ears and took a breath. He felt lonely suddenly, for the other parts of his mind were silent, and though he knew the robot was a simple thing, its artificial voice had banished for a few minutes the oppressive, uncanny silence of the colony.

He brought up his wrist computer, unable to ignore that it was past 12:00 hours, and flipped through his messages.

"Did you instigate this, Saul Toro?" he said to himself, wondering about the vague language used by his employer. He tapped his head. "I need to get you all wrangled. I'm pretty blind for a man who can see the past and future."

His inner self answered back, but it was the remnant of his original mind, not the part of him that was prescient or able to see into the past. It was laughing with pleasure – a cackle that was somehow also guttural and strained. Andrew shut it out.

The lift slowed as it pulled into a corridor hewn into the rock. A pair of black composite doors swung open as the car pushed against them, revealing a tighter tunnel with the lift rail running through it. Air began to whistle all around the car, but stopped when the black doors closed again. The lift stopped, swaying slightly, and Andrew saw out the window a small foyer opening up into workspaces much like those in the residential area. Computer stations sat at desks, but none of them were on. Rather than sodium lights, the space was lit by bright white diodes running in the corners of the hallways, which, though unfinished, were nonetheless quite square.

At last, the door opened and Andrew stepped out. Immediately he lifted his rifle and checked his left and his right, making sure he was alone. He quickly grabbed his nose and forced his ears to pop again. There wasn't an additional atmosphere generator running in the space, he realized. He took a deep breath, thinking that he should have been more cautious and worn his full suit. With a sigh, he stepped through the foyer to the workspace beyond.

It was large and sparse, a remote office made to serve the technical and logistics needs of the current progress zone. The dead computer monitors reflected back the subtle white of the ambient lighting, looking like a dozen frozen faces with white slits for eyes. Past the workspaces were more hallways. Andrew stepped toward these, checking around each desk, wondering if he would see a body lying behind one, or perhaps a living person. He saw nothing but dusty wires and refuse. The robots which maintained the living spaces of the colony had obviously yet to reach this distant place.

Still, that's a lot of trash, he said to himself, wondering at the piles of forgotten papers and wrappers. A chill ran up his spine as his boots slid over the slick floor caked with rough dust, and for a moment, he heard laughter, almost audible. He ignored it.

Andrew stepped toward a hallway, where the running lights thinned to a single strip in one rough-hewn corner. He resisted the urge to flip on his flashlight, and instead stepped softly into the dim corridor. A few yards in he saw a fork. One path, lit by old lights on a rough stair, went down to a space filled with orange sodium lights. The other wound forward, and he could see more white light there.

He tried asking himself what he could expect with each one, but his prescient mind gave no response.

He turned to go to the mine first. He began to feel sweat breaking on his brow as he descended. The steps were irregular, some short, some steep, and many of them much longer than stairs normally were, so he got deeper only slowly. The white lights of the office began to dim behind him, replaced by the eerie flickering orange of high-pressure sodium.

He held his breath as his foot stepped and slipped on something. He flipped on the light attached to the forward lug of his rifle, refusing the detached caution that begged him not to, and looked down. There was a pile of food going down several steps. Most of it was unopened, still sitting in its clear cellophane wrappers as if waiting for someone to buy it from a machine. In other places, the food was ripped open and half-eaten.

Andrew wondered if the food was piled up from the bottom or thrown down from the top. He decided that nobody would go so far down the steps just to toss unopened food, and so he carefully stepped his way through it until he reached the landing. Before him was a wide mining zone. Tunnels reinforced with steel ran in many different directions, some up, some down. Tracks ran out of most of these.

Robotic haulers stood idle in a line to the side, most of them looking broken or forgotten. Some of the tunnels were still lit in the same orange, but most were dark.

Peeling his eyes from the maze in front of him, Andrew looked down at his wrist computer. He searched for a wireless network, but could find none. *I guess the office was shut down, along with the network. But then, Lucille was still active…*

He looked at the time, wondering if the loss of network would reset it. It read close to 13:00. He shrugged and stepped toward one of the tunnels, meaning to see how far down it went.

He forgot his train of thought as a vision assaulted him.

He was in one of the corridors. A light flickered just behind him. Two people appeared from the darkness, rising from an unlit tunnel he hadn't seen. They were too quick for him. All he could see was their faces – ashen in the monochromatic lights, thin-skinned and pale. Their mouths were exceptionally large and twisted into strange grimaces over teeth that were over-long from the withering of their dark gums. He fired his rifle into nothingness, then the vision began to fade as he felt hands pushing into his stomach, parting the flesh, seeking something inside him. Dozens of wriggling fingers, like the tentacles of some vicious squid twisting his insides towards a beaked maw…

He was staring at the tunnel again. Around a bend, he saw a flickering light. Calming himself with a slow breath, he stepped into the tunnel.

Each time he was assaulted with a vision of his death, he had to make a decision – run away, or use the knowledge to confront and hopefully avoid his demise. He didn't always decide to face his fear, but more often than not he trusted the optionality of the vision, especially since he had regained his old proficiency with his weapons. He supposed that in the abandoned mine that, should he inspect another path, the monsters he saw could approach him from another angle – an angle he hadn't yet foreseen.

The vision held steady in his mind as he walked along the cart track, letting Andrew know that he was proceeding toward the finality of it; had he walked away, the vision would begin to evaporate like a dream, being no longer part of the future. He saw the flickering light, its ballast failing after untold hours of steady work. He brought his sights up to his right eye as he approached the empty space from his vision.

It was a space of nothingness, easily overlooked as part of the endless colorless dark stone. As he pointed his flashlight into the void, he saw movement. Two heads turned to look at him, their eyes wide and reflective like those of a cat. Attached to those heads were two malformed bodies, withered but also smooth; colorless or so covered with filth as be robbed of the hues of flesh. They were hunched over something, but Andrew could not see what.

He only regarded them for a fleeting second, then he opened fire, knowing they would kill him if he did not. He started with two quick shots to the central mass of each. Black blood sprayed out in clouds, but they initially seemed little affected. Screaming in chillingly low tones, making a dissonant diad between them, they burst from their lair. Andrew's pulse quickened as they flailed about, bumping into each other recklessly, falling over themselves while black blood and bile spilled from their open ribs.

Andrew fired slowly and deliberately, willing his nerves to obey him. Two bullets hammered through the heads of the attackers, and their progress finally stopped. Seemingly unwilling to accept the loss of the brain, their bodies continued to try to run as they toppled over and collapsed. Long fingers terminating in jagged nails whipped about. Andrew stepped closer and tapped another shot into each head, watching as the bodies finally began to stop moving.

He approached the closest and flipped it over. The body was human in some ways essential to the species, containing all the bones and structure of a normal person. The skin was grey under the white diodes of his flashlight. It was also slightly translucent, revealing the anatomy beneath: tendons and muscle fascia, bone and sinew and long, blue veins. Remnants of clothing still clung to their bodies. He knelt closer, but could not see anything immediately identifiable on either one.

They were human once, which meant that the creatures were the colonists. Nobody else had been to the desolate ferrous planet before him.

Andrew stepped over the bodies and looked closer into the little hiding hole from which the monsters had emerged. Tattered clothing was everywhere, like a nest. The remnants of a half-rotten body were present, torn into pieces that were only vaguely human. Andrew guessed at where the rest of the corpse had gone.

He checked his computer and quickly punched in a message. He was too deep now to transmit directly back to his ship, but as soon as he was in communications range the message would go out, informing Toro of what he had seen, and warning him that nobody else should be sent. He quickly turned and half-jogged back toward the central chamber, happy to cut his mission short and negotiate with his employer for payment even though he had failed to find his mark.

Another vision hit him, though this one did not totally blank out his sight, as those further in the future usually did.

He saw two more of the monsters waiting for him in the central chamber. He gunned them down, only to be floored by an attacker from above.

Andrew focused as he went around the bend. He dropped to a knee as soon as he saw the brightly lit central room. Two shadowy figures were there. He shot each of them. Like the others, these began to charge at him, but he could see through their odd movements that his rifle was indeed effective at injuring them, they were just more reluctant to die than a regular person. He continued to fire as they slowly collapsed to the ground, just to be sure. Then he saw the hidden attacker emerge – along with two others.

They ran at him quickly, their gate unmistakably human, though it became more monstrous as they were hit, turning into a knuckle walk or a fast crawl.

Andrew's bolt snapped back and stopped. Smoke rose from the empty chamber. He dropped his magazine and slammed in another. He let the bolt fly forward and continued firing at his attackers, which had closed the distance more quickly than he thought possible. Fear gripped him at that moment, and he let himself shoot more wildly than he knew was wise. The loss of discipline didn't matter. Soon all three lay in twitching heaps five yards ahead of him.

"Thanks, mate," Andrew said tapping his left fist to his temple. Before walking on, he took out his magazine and quickly checked to see how many rounds he had left, since in the moment he had forgotten to count. Seeing eight remaining, he tucked away the magazine and put in a full one. He picked up his spent magazine from the floor and put it away too, then walked slowly down the hallway, keeping his rifle trained on the bodies in front of him, whose nerves still fired in defiance of the very real death of the major organs.

Like the others, they were people – at least at one time. One of the closer ones seemed less monstrous than the others. It was a woman, likely young-looking whenever what changed her had taken hold. Her hair was still black, though matted, and though her skin was thin and stretched, he could still see healthy fat around the lips and cheeks. She still wore her clothes – a simple set of coveralls.

Something occurred to Andrew. He had been so focused on the idea that there was a *Wrtla* at play that he had not considered other causes. Had some sort of pathogen his sensors could not detect caused this? Should he have resisted the urge to remove his helmet and breathe the air of the place? He looked at his computer and started up the air filter on his suit. Within a few moments, it returned a safe value. No atypical pathogens. DNA mutations in microbes within normal limits.

Andrew opened his mind briefly to the oldest part of himself, and heard the laughing internally, drawing fingers towards his lips to pull them into a smile. He pushed it away.

It has to be a Wrtla. I need to get out of here, payments be damned.

He stepped over the bodies and continued to the central room of the mine, piquing his prescient self for warnings, but none came. The dead in the central room were in a similar state to the woman – still dressed and looking far less gone than the first pair he had slain. He turned and looked above to the tunnel from which he had just exited to see a small platform attached to the steel scaffolding.

They were smart enough to set a trap for me, once they knew I was here.

He headed back toward the stairway. He stepped over the pile of uneaten pre-packaged food and continued back up, still keeping his rifle ready, in case he needed it. At the top of the stairs, he turned to the left, seeing a pale white glow from another finished workspace. As he turned a sharp corner, his past mind, his echo mind, jumped forward, almost displacing his normal thoughts, but seemed unable to complete its normal vision process.

He saw a wide office space that was in shambles. Phantoms of people in tattered clothes moved toward him, their eyes wide and reflecting the fluorescent lights above in a pale green. At the same time, he saw the space as it was – desks were neat and ordered, and people stood about talking and working. Several of the desks were actually workbenches, piled with parts and other machines that were being fixed.

His mind splintered again, and he saw the figures with the pale eyes moving toward him, almost like ghosts, and saw himself shooting them down, one at a time with clear precision. They began to move in the present, and he enacted the will of his future self, slaughtering the wraiths as they fumbled their way over the ruined floor, looking more confused than angry.

Somehow he held onto sanity as he heard the laughing of that other part of his mind, which held the taint of an eternal demon as well as most of his human memories. He was pressing forward, demanding to take part in the sanguine feast, and there was another voice with him, singing a horrid song into his ear.

There were three images competing with the laughter – past, present, and future. His prescient mind saw something that gave him pause. He shot and killed, amidst the throng, a young woman who, he realized only too late, looked totally normal. She was a single image standing in all three places; only the future image was frozen, blood flying out from a wound in her neck, surprise plastered on her pale face.

He took his finger off the trigger, rather than following through with the prescribed motions of the future, and suddenly the future vision changed, then winked out of sight. He was nearly set upon by four people, two of them walking and two of them crawling forward, strange words in an alien tongue spilling from their mouths like linguistic vomit. Andrew glanced up and saw the girl, who stood still and stared at him. Her eyes were almost glassy, but trembled, as if in fear.

He blinked hard, then quickly dispatched the remaining attackers.

Brass tinkled on the stone floor, then all was silent, save for a moaning, wracking sound coming from one of the mad people. Andrew stepped toward the victim, intending to put it to final rest, when a wordless cry from the girl stopped him in his tracks.

He looked up at her. She cried out again, as if trying to form words, but the utterance came out slurred and strange.

Andrew held out his left palm and lowered his rifle.

The woman stepped quickly toward him. Andrew resisted the temptation to gun her down, remembering the vision, and stepped back. He watched as she went to the wheezing wretch on the ground. She pushed it over to reveal a middle-aged man. He looked like some of the others: pale and thin-skinned, but human besides the strange, hollow eyes.

The young woman shook the man, then stood up, almost defiantly against his armed bulk. She was crying, and Andrew watched as she grabbed a piece of her simple grey shirt and blotted her tears. Despite the grit caked on her face and in her hair, she looked young. Andrew thought she wouldn't pass for 20 Earth years. She stomped her foot as she looked at him, and her pouty expression was almost childish, though below it was something harder than any youth should possess. Andrew wondered how old she really was.

"Can you understand me?" Andrew said, still not raising his rifle, though his trigger finger was of two minds, dancing on and off while his thumb toggled the safety randomly.

She nodded. Her frown deepened as she pointed to the dead man at her feet.

"Can you talk?"

She nodded, but at the same time, wordless vocalizations came out of her mouth.

"I can't understand you."

The girl clenched her fists and grunted.

"You knew him?" Andrew said.

She nodded.

"Sorry. There was nothing for it. He would have killed me." Andrew frowned. "You must be early in the change, but why?" he said, mostly to himself. "Everyone else is far gone. Too far gone to save. Are you… yourself?"

He saw that she was staring at him, but was unsure if she was comprehending. His trigger finger danced some more. He realized that his echo mind – hearing some voice of the past, was still trying to push a vision forward. He allowed it more room, and he saw the workspace as it was, with the strange girl seated at a nearby desk, writing in a notebook. Somebody was seated across from her, talking to her, but the vision was silent. The girl's lips didn't move.

Andrew snapped out of it as the girl stepped past him. He flinched, but he realized she wasn't attacking. She was searching for something in the rubble. She knelt down and retrieved a simple notebook. A pen was perched on the back cover, and she took it, then opened the notebook and began writing with her right hand. She turned it toward him.

I'm normal, it said in jagged letters.

"I'm not so sure of that," Andrew said. "There's a *Wrtla* at work here. You've clearly been affected, but maybe if I got you out of here right away-"

She frowned at him and waved her hands, then said with great effort, "No." She pointed at the notebook again.

Andrew shook his head. She grabbed at his arm, and he reflexively shrank away, fumbling with his rifle before lowering it again. Once again, she pointed at the notebook.

Andrew took a breath and paused. He looked carefully at the girl. He noticed a subtle disturbance in her face, as if half of it was not under control, though not quite drooping like someone who had suffered a stroke. He tilted his head and saw a slight scar running through her scalp to her neck behind her right ear.

"You've had a head injury..." he whispered, craning his head to see. She caught sight of him examining her, and leaned her head, cupping a hand over her right ear.

"I said you've been injured. Recently?"

She shook her head. Sudden realization dawned on her face, and she reached into her pocket with her right hand. She fumbled out a wallet from her trousers, almost dropping it as she opened it up. She handed Andrew a plain white card.

Andrew had to hold the card up in the dim lights, but was able to read:

My name is Mariela Flores. I have suffered a traumatic brain injury. I have difficulty with certain physical tasks, including speech. I may have difficulty understanding you or communicating my thoughts accurately. Janice Telany is my therapist and can be paged over the network. She can program my AAC device with new conversations.

Andrew looked back at the girl. "Nice to meet you. I'm Andrew. Or… Andrew is the right-now me." He shrugged. "What happened to your communications device?"

Mariela waved her hands as if trying to sign something, shrugged, then bent her notebook in the middle.

"We need to get you out of here."

She shook her head, then scribbled on her notebook. *My parents are still here.*

Andrew nodded in understanding. That's why her neuroanatomy remained unrepaired. She must have been younger when it happened, and there were no transports to take her back to a settled planet with proper facilities. Or perhaps the damage was beyond repair. He touched his own head.

"No fixing me," he said aloud. "But you *do* need to leave. I might have already killed your parents."

Mariela frowned deeply at him, then rushed past him, back toward the hallway and the mine.

"Wait!" Andrew shouted. "There could be-"

Before he could finish his sentence, his future mind pressed forward, demanding his attention. A swarm of insane people was emerging from the tunnels in the mine, rushing toward where he stood in the vision. He saw Mariela, who he was chasing. They paid her no mind, pushing past her on both sides. Then he saw an empty liquid gas tank tip over at the passing of some clumsy madwoman, and fall onto Mariela, stunning her.

Andrew was frozen in his decision as the vision of himself being smothered by bodies began to fade. The former workers seemed to ignore the girl – for what reason he could not guess, though he suspected some familiarity that persisted despite the stupefied state – but at the same time, she was in real danger. He broke his paralysis and ran after Mariela.

Fear began to tighten his throat, and he broke into a sweat in his temperature-regulated suit. Normally, his future visions gave him something tangible to avoid, or could guide him in some way, but this one gave him only his demise. He supposed as he ran down the hallway, following the echo of footsteps, that he could turn back and avoid the situation entirely, but he felt a stronger duty to persist. Mariela could be saved, he was sure.

He began down the stairwell, trying his best to avoid slipping on the remnants of old food wrappers. He heard the sound of more footsteps, and knew the horde, likely awakened by his scuffle earlier, was inbound. The lights in the stairwell flickered and went out. He was in near-total darkness; the only light was from behind him, but below him, his own shadow blocked all. He flipped on the flashlight on his bottom lug rail.

He fell backward with the shock, hitting the stone stairs heavily. Below him was a swarm of people groping forward, climbing over one of their number that was struggling on the bottom stair.

"Hold him! Hold him!" came one of their voices from the noisy din, and Andrew knew this lot, though clearly mad, was cognizant enough to be something more dangerous than a herd of animals. Their mouths were twisted and wide, their skin pale and taught, but a dark light was in their eyes, which refracted and defied the blinding whiteness of the gun's light even as their pupils drank it up.

Andrew's nerves unwound; he hadn't been surprised – truly surprised – in a very long time. Without thought, he squeezed the trigger of his rifle, firing a single shot into the stone wall that went ricocheting down the stairwell. His earplugs deadened the sound immediately, but the cognizant insane humans before him lacked such tactical protection.

They screamed and wailed in unison. It was a sickening sound to Andrew, but it gave him time to hastily flip the safety over to auto and fire wildly into the throng of attackers.

Blood sprayed up onto his suit. Onto his face. The warmth of it sickened him, shattering his resolve even as it brought howling laughter from within. The screaming intensified. The bolt locked open. With trembling fingers, Andrew dropped the magazine and slammed in another. He tried to master himself, watching the remaining bodies in the bright circle of light in front of him. He fired another burst – perhaps ten rounds – into the motion before him, then forced himself to toggle back to semi. The light trembled before him, and he willed it to stay still. The bodies below him were still or sliding backward. There were fewer than there ought to have been, meaning that some had fled, surely awaiting him down below, if he dared to try to retrieve the girl.

He took a breath and slowly worked his way downward, avoiding the bleeding bodies. One still twitched – its face contorted and ticking around vacuous, dead eyes. The image seemed to burn into Andrew's retinas, a memory at which his old self seemed to smile inwardly.

Near the bottom of the stairwell, his future mind kicked in again, revealing the waiting attack from both his right and left, the madmen hiding behind piles of discarded equipment. In the vision he saw the remaining group standing back, fearful near one of the tunnels.

As the vision faded, Andrew's present mind quickly formulated a strategy. He reached to his back and retrieved his plasma gun. He balanced its considerable girth in his left hand and quickly double-checked the battery life. The indicator on its white-metal case glowed a bright green. It was a clever death tool, compact and efficient, but he didn't trust it in an atmosphere unless he had no choice.

He stepped out into the open cavern and pointed his guns out to his left and right. Looking ahead to find the rest of his enemies, he fired a burst from each gun blindly. The roar of the plasma gun almost overwhelmed the loud rifle, its energy ripping apart the nitrogen and oxygen in the atmosphere at a molecular level, but the report from each weapon indicated impact with flesh. He saw the remaining miners, then glanced left and right to see a dead man on each side. The one on his left was burned nearly black and smoking. The stink sent a wave of nausea over him, but his old self suddenly pushed a finger of insanity up into Andrew's psyche, which quelled the need to vomit and hardened him temporarily.

Andrew dropped his plasma gun, letting it hang around his shoulder by its bungee strap, then sighted the last group. They were rushing at him, ignoring Mariela as if she were an inanimate object, though she reached out her hands as if trying to stop and slow them. They swarmed around, knocking the girl roughly down, paying her no notice.

Andrew was back in control now, and he didn't need the faint early images from his prescient mind to tell him what to shoot. He carefully executed each rushing man and woman, tapping each one in the chest twice. Six fell as they ran. Ten. Twelve. The last one took one shot in the shoulder, and the rifle was empty. Andrew let go of the rifle and picked up his plasma gun. The man was almost upon him, blood pouring from his single wound. Andrew could see his face – which was both confused and angry.

With two air-burning shots, Andrew obliterated the man, turning him into a smoking corpse with two gaping wounds seared through him. The man's face was plastered in a slightly sad expression as he fell. Andrew had a flashback; he saw the man sitting near Mariela in an office, talking calmly. The girl seemed not to notice the conversation, and stared at her hands.

"Mariela, let's go!" Andrew said. "You see you can't stay here. He was mad. They all were, and I can tell you, there is no cure."

Mariela picked herself up, shocked at the carnage surrounding her. Tears were welling in her open, trembling eyes.

Andrew gave her an appraising stare. He looked down at the blood, which was running between the forgotten prepackaged snacks piled at the bottom of the stairs. His mind was blank, unable to think of the next step as he looked upon the gory horror of his handiwork. The stoic lane that he piloted his psyche through was suddenly no longer straight, but was like a winding path. He felt no immediate disgust, or fear, but all around him the feelings pressed in. All he really knew was that he had to escape the sight; escape, or else succumb and lose what control he still held.

Hesitantly, willing his voice to work, he said, "I'm… going to the elevators." His voice died like sand spilling on stone. He choked slightly. Silently, he considered carrying Mariela out by force, but the warm liquid running underfoot unnerved him. He turned and walked hurriedly up the stairs, gripping the handrail on his left in case he slipped in the blood, which was running in torrents over the stone steps. In some places, the puddles on the uneven stairs were deep enough to lap over the tops of his composite boots. He let his rifle slide to behind his right hip and continued holding his plasma gun in his right hand; he wanted the escape from the grizzly scene even more than he wanted to reload, for it was more than a sight, it was a beacon, and he feared the one who would heed it – the one who laughed in the cold recesses between his footsteps.

When he reached the top of the stairs he traded his weapons, traded his magazine for a fresh one, then started back toward the lift, refusing to turn and watch the stairs.

As he walked, another part of his mind pushed forward with a vision, though he couldn't be sure which. He was sitting alone in the cockpit of his ship, calm and without fear. It faded as he neared the lift car, dissipating into hazy memory as quickly as it had come.

It stood open, just as he had left it, a lighthouse to the floundering ship of his mind, beaten by waves of emotion. He reached the control terminal and sighed, leaning against the wall. He looked out at the track through the lift car window, watching it fade into night. The running lights disappeared into the twisting rock further out, hiding the points beyond. He could not bear to wonder what was out there, which was just as well, as he had decided he would leave without finding his mark. He simply could not endure any longer.

The girl he was supposed to find was just that – a girl, and he had thus far seen only adults, save for Mariela, who hardly qualified as such. The children were likely dead – he had a sudden echo of the horror on the first floor, along with laughter from his old self – or else were in the sixth sector, along with the rest of the colonists. And their minds were surely gone. He turned and looked back at the empty space of the landing and the tunnel to the mine. Mariela had not followed him.

He looked at the panel and considered leaving Mariela, but despite the emotional detachment he had developed over the fractured months, he felt horror at the threat of guilt of such a decision. Guilt in the moment washed over him, as he considered that he left her amid his carnage, as if she were a child throwing a tantrum, refusing to come when bidden, not a grown woman who had witnessed the death of a dozen people she had known since childhood. And she had not followed. Of course! She would not leave, not if she would walk headstrong into the hive of monsters without a care.

Andrew banged his fist against his head. "What's wrong with you?" He stepped away from the elevator, hearing a beep from his computer, alerting him to an unexpected jump in his blood pressure and pulse. He reached the stairwell, whose lights were now flickering, threatening to return to some semblance of life. To his relief, Mariela was walking up the stairs. In the high contrast of the flickering lights he could almost pretend the floor was black, not crimson. Caked with oil, rather than blood.

"I'm glad you're coming," he said.

She raised her eyes to look at him, and frowned with anger.

"I'm sorry," he said, and stepped back to let her pass. She turned back toward the office and began walking quickly.

"The elevators are back this way," he said. She ignored him. He sighed. He would have to carry her out after all. Leaving her would be unacceptable. Horrific. He started after her. When he reached the office space, he found Mariela emptying some drawers and pulling out various items from beneath an aluminum desk, then stuffing them into a backpack. She pulled out a sponge cake from the bag, opened the wrapper and bit down into it, and then walked toward Andrew.

Andrew frowned with realization. "You got everything?"

Mariela nodded, then walked past him, eating the snack cake noisily. Andrew skipped a step to keep up.

"It was you that left all that food at the bottom of the stairs."

She glanced at him and nodded.

"Why?"

She put the snack cake in her mouth and rubbed her stomach.

Andrew thought a moment. "You came here and left it for the... people, below?"

She nodded.

"They stopped eating the food."

She nodded again.

"But you kept coming down here anyway."

Mariela continued to nod.

"You got it from the main dormitories. That's why so many machines were empty."

She looked at him and nodded curtly.

"If you could have put out the beacon for help the whole time, why didn't you?" He remembered and corrected himself, "Unless you didn't know how to pull the alarm or-"

Mariela shook her head and then pointed to her temple.

"You didn't because you didn't want to lose your parents?" He shook his head. "Oh, it's probably better you didn't call for help. Whoever came would be enslaved..." Andrew trailed off and looked hard at Mariela.

She didn't respond to his monologue. She walked quickly to the elevator and began working the computer terminal outside it. The doors opened.

"Willing to leave now?"

Mariela stared at him. She finished the last of the cake, then scribbled in her notebook and showed it to Andrew.

They won't come out now. They haven't eaten food in a long time.

"There are more people down there still, hiding?"

She nodded.

"Do your parents notice you? Do they acknowledge you?"

Mariela looked sadly at him and shook her head.

"It's the *wrtla*. What they were... they're gone."

Mariela scribbled. *I know.* Then, *What's a wertala?*

"*Wrtla*," Andrew said, trying to drop the vowels and pronounce the title he had learned from his contact with... he could not remember its proper name, just it's title. He motioned to the elevator. Mariela stepped in and he followed. He watched her punch up the dormitories. The car started moving, lurching from its resting place, squeaking as it slowly began its ascent.

Mariela pointed again to her notebook. *What's a Wertala?*

Andrew thought a moment. "It's an ancient monster. A demon, a devil." He shook his head. "Something beyond such concepts – they don't do it justice. It can control the minds of humans, turn them mad. It eats sanity like its food. A long time ago – nobody who knows anything about the *wrtla* knows exactly how long but we think close to a hundred thousand Earth years – they were imprisoned by a race of beings that could compete with their power. Angels, maybe, but they left nothing behind. The *wrtla* were placed deep within planets like this one, hopefully to be forgotten by man. Whatever they are, my guess is they are immortal on some level, but clearly not powerful enough to escape a prison of rock.

"But their powers can leak through, touching the minds of people. Maybe they've been coming through for a long time. Calling mankind down, back to them – some primeval song without words or melody. We hear it between the words of thought. Out in space..." Andrew was clenching his hands as he talked. "They can whisper, too, if you get too close, and once they get in, you'll be their slave, and if you escape, you'll go mad. Trust me, I know."

He was waiting for her to ask him how he knew. He dreaded the question, because within it was the explanation of his power, but also of the madman that lurked within him, ready to take control and wreak havoc. He laughed inside (and not the "old" Andrew) – *madman! Ha!* – he was already a madman, with four minds living inside him, constantly trying to be the one true mind, constantly talking behind each other's backs. Some part of him wanted her to ask him. He needed confession. He longed for it.

But she didn't ask him. Instead, she wrote in her notebook again.

I haven't heard any whispers. I'm not insane.

"You'd have to be a little crazy to keep coming down to feed those people," Andrew said.

She wrote, *What else should I have done?*

Andrew shrugged. "Did any of the others acknowledge you? Notice your existence?"

She shook her head.

"Weird. I think the unprotected part of my mind can hear the thing inside the rock whispering, practically screaming. Or singing."

What is it saying?

Andrew opened up to his old self for a few moments. "Lots of things. Kill, mostly. But you don't have to worry about me. Like I said, it only whispers to the unprotected part of my mind, and it's locked away safely." Andrew bit his lip. He did need confession. He made up his mind to see a priest when he got out of this, though he wondered if the priest would understand, and would actually be willing to help him pray; help him find forgiveness.

Old Andrew was balking at him at the thought. *A priest? You think he knows God*

The car rocked as it passed a beam in the dark.

Mariela scribbled, *Why did you come here? To get me?*

"No. But I won't leave someone behind who can be saved."

She pointed at the notebook again.

"I came to save a little girl named Vivian Toro. I was hired by her father, Saul Toro. I don't think I'll be able to finish the job, though."

I know her. Little girl.

"She's probably dead by now."

I wasn't dead.

"You're immune, that is, if you really don't hear the voice. You're an adult… If Vivian was immune, there was nobody to care for her."

Mariela frowned and then wrote quickly, *You're a coward.*

Andrew flushed slightly. "I can't feasibly search every cranny of this mine. It's not possible as one man."

You know she's on level six. The rest are.

"I don't know that."

Mariela touched the panel and the lift car stopped, swinging in the abyss. She pointed to the notebook again.

"I have a responsibility to *you* now. I must see you to safety first."

She sighed as she wrote. *I was already safe.*

"You won't be if I head to level six."

They don't pay attention to me. She was getting tearful as she pointed to her words. She grunted in exasperation and went to the panel. The car started moving back. Andrew saw she had punched in level six. He sighed and stepped over, but she slapped his hand as he reached for the panel. Quickly, she unplugged it from the wall.

"I can just plug the monitor back in."

She shook her head. She wrote again.

I know the way.

Andrew sighed. He remembered her standing still while the vile people of the mind swarmed past her, bent on him. Perhaps she was right, and they would ignore her. "Where is the closest security station? Any weapons storage?"

Mariela smiled asymmetrically. The left side of her face seemed unwilling to go with the rest. She kneeled down and plugged the monitor back in. With a few strokes, they were headed back up.

Andrew leaned back and looked at Mariela. She stood looking out the window as they moved through the darkness, the lights on the rails making an endlessly extending road to nowhere. The girl looked terrified, but at the same time without fear. A sadness touched her eyes, which seemed fixed in a downturned expression. Andrew could not be sure if that was due to some neurological damage, or if she was emoting into the abyss.

"Do you know how to operate a gun?"

Mariela turned and looked at him. She nodded once. Andrew doubted that was a true answer, but the question on its own was a gambit he could not back out of.

"If I die, take the elevator back to the dormitories. My ship is parked outside. You won't be able to operate it without an access code, but there is a distress beacon on board that will function. I have a few friends in the sector that know I'm here. They'll take care of you, but don't let them into the colony."

Mariela looked at him as if to say thanks, but all that came out were some confused vocalizations. She sighed and wrote in her notebook.

You think you will die?

"It's always a possibility. If I see something we can't avoid, we'll just leave."

What if they surprise you?

Andrew smiled. "I'm difficult to surprise. Make sure you pay attention to me and obey my orders."

She nodded.

The lift reached the sector four landing station and slowed. It was dusty and the bright lights of the robot Lucille could be seen down a long hallway.

"Anyone on this level?" Andrew said as the doors opened.

Mariela shrugged.

"Do you know where the weapons locker is?"

Mariela bit her lip.

"Do you know that there is one on this level?"

She nodded.

"Lucille ought to know, then. That's that robot up ahead."

He stepped out into the cavernous foyer and flipped on his light. He swung through the still hanging dust, checking corners, then waved Mariela forward. They went straight down the half-finished hallway toward the working robot. They passed a few doors that Andrew hastily checked for any signs of humans, then finally reached Lucille.

The robot ceased kicking up the dust and cleaning the floor as they approached.

"Hello, Toro," the robot said in a kindly voice. "It's good to see you again. Is your shift over?"

"Not quite," Andrew said. "Do you know where security is on this level?"

"Has there been an incident?"

Andrew paused a moment. "Yes."

Lucille clicked silently, its dimmed flashlight head motionless. "There are no security personnel on active duty in this sector. Shall I page another station?"

"It won't do any good," Andrew said.

"Why not? Is something wrong with the security personnel?"

Andrew looked at Mariela, who shrugged.

"The network is malfunctioning," Andrew said. "The
personnel are on duty, but… but all of the stations are…"
He stammered as his past self begged for his attention, raving, but also pleading. He listened for a brief second. "The
system software is bugged out and is returning a null value
for all members of the team. I need to get to the station to
correct it, but I'm new here."

Lucille clicked again. Its head turned and seemed to regard Mariela. "You can reach the closest security station by
returning to the lift terminals, taking the second hallway
from the left, and proceeding to room three, on the left.
Greetings, Mariela."

Mariela nodded nervously to the robot.

"Have a nice day, Lucille," Andrew said. He grabbed
Mariela's hand lightly and led her away from the robot, back
down toward the lifts. They quickly made the rounds and
found room three, which had a clear gold-lettered sign read-
ing "Security."

As Andrew reached for the door handle, he had a slight
premonition. It wasn't a full-blown vision, but his prescient
self was warning him, though not of imminent danger. With
the echo of the forgotten crib, he had some idea what to expect.

The door, however, did not wish to open. Looking
around, Andrew saw that it was a powered lock, and the
power had been disconnected at some point.

"Damn, Lucille, why did you have to clean before fixing
anything?" He looked at Mariela. "Stand over there."

Andrew took his plasma gun out and covered his eyes with his arm before obliterating the door lock. Pieces of aluminum shrapnel spun away, bouncing off of his suit and the wall. White smoke billowed up, but the fire system didn't recognize it. Andrew kicked the door in, which gave easily. The rest of the lock rattled off and clanged on the ground.

The lights flickered on as they entered. It was a rather normal office for a large mining operation's minimally-needed security, containing generic furniture, computers, seating, and a few lockers. Andrew saw immediately what his prescient self had warned him of. Lying down against one of the walls was a man in the remains of a security uniform. He was clearly dead, his eyes drawn and opaque, his flesh withered slightly and desiccated. His peeled lips were thin and revealed rotting gums holding long teeth.

Surprisingly, it only stunk slightly.

"He must have died of thirst, having forgotten how to get out," Andrew said. He stepped around the corpse to one of the lockers. He found it unlocked, to his surprise. "Any preference?" he said to Mariela, gesturing at the open locker. She was standing aghast at the sight of the dead man, her mouth open and eyes trembling.

Andrew snapped his fingers at her until she looked at him. "Sorry you had to see that. I forgot to tell you to expect something like that."

She gave him a puzzled look.

"Now. Do you have a weapon preference?" He gestured again at the open locker, which contained an assortment of small arms.

Mariela shook her head, clearly confused.

Andrew nodded slightly to her. He took a twelve gauge shotgun out and placed it on a nearby table, then looked through some drawers and found the ammunition. After some searching, he found a few boxes of buckshot and put them on the table too. Next, he found in a drawer a 9 millimeter pistol. He saw that it was locked to an electronic security bracelet. He brought it to the table and quickly took it down. Using a multi-tool from his belt, he pried out the identity device that was attached to the trigger group and threw it away, chuckling. The slide went back on, and he tested the trigger, watching the hammer move smoothly through the long action double-action.

He put in a magazine and racked the slide, then eased the hammer down. He made to hand it to Mariela, then withdrew it. A thought had just occurred to him

If she's invisible to the Wrtla, will I be able to see a future where she intends to kill me? He remembered all the people he had slaughtered in the other sector. What if he had already killed her parents, and she was looking for revenge?

He saw that Mariela was looking at him questioningly, clearly not understanding what was going on his head.

I saw her in the vision… was that just incidental?

His past self pushed forward *You saw her in the past.*

But…

He sighed and handed the pistol to Mariela, barrel first in case she tried to shoot him. He held his breath as she looked at it with half familiarity. She placed it in her right hand and weighed it.

"That's just your sidearm." Andrew turned back and found a few loaded magazines. He slid them across to the girl, who stuffed one of them in her pants pocket and the rest in her backpack. "Your main gun ought to be this," he said, picking up the shotgun. He found the bolt release and pressed it down, then racked the bolt a few times, ejecting what he knew were beanbag rounds. He opened up one of the boxes of buckshot and loaded eight fresh shells in the magazine, then dropped one in the open chamber. He released the bolt and it slammed closed. He held it to Mariela, who took it doubtingly. "Put the rest of the ammo in your backpack."

She nodded and put down the shotgun carefully. She then put the extra shells into a pocket on the outside of her backpack.

"You sure you know how to use it?"

Mariela nodded and picked up the gun. Her left hand held the foregrip uneasily, but as she rested the stock on her hip, it settled down. Andrew nodded slowly. Keeping the girl in his periphery, he turned back, checking the rifles in the locker. They were all chambered in 6.2 millimeter, not his old rifle's 6.8. He shook the satchel at his hip, feeling the weight. It was light. He put his hand in and felt three more loaded magazines. Normally he would feel fine with ninety rounds, but his prescient mind was whistling at him.

With a sigh, he picked up one of the security rifles and popped open the receiver. With his multi-tool, he removed the electronic security block on the auto-sear and tossed it aside. He slung the rifle around him, annoyed that it lacked a more ready suspension system, like the bungees that held his main rifle. A quick search of the gun locker found a whole drawer full of pre-loaded magazines, along with a few empties. He put them in his satchel, feeling suddenly very weighed down, even in the lower gravity of the colony.

"After you," he said, pointing to the open door. He watched Mariela exit and turn down toward the elevators.

They reached them and stepped inside. Andrew put his own rifle down, leaning it against a corner to retrieve on the trip back. Mariela fumbled with the shotgun slightly, leaning it next to his rifle. She brought the terminal to life, and the lift car was soon moving back through the dark, toward sector six.

"You don't have to come too, you know. You could wait for me at the dorms."

Mariela stared at him, then wrote slowly, *I'm not afraid. Are you?*

"Yeah. The me that's *me* is. The me that sees the future, not so much, which should be reassuring, but I don't trust him. He doesn't answer a lot of questions."

She looked at him with a puzzled expression.

"I have a few residents upstairs. They're all me. One lives in the future, one lives in the past, one lives in *my* past, but I don't talk to him much."

Mariela wrote on her pad, *Are you insane?*

Andrew paused and ran his tongue over his teeth. "That's what a doctor would say, but I'm still alive, and most wouldn't be who have tread the paths I have. Paths like this one."

Mariela stared at him.

"Where do you think a kid would be in sector six?"

She shook her head.

Andrew took a slow breath.

The car slid on in silence, eventually approaching the landing for sector five. Andrew could see several shapes moving amid the lights, scattering as the car approached. They slid through, and all that could be seen were a few pair of vacuous, open eyes watching them pass.

The running lights along the track were brighter here, and the space through which the lift moved was less uncomfortably open. They passed through open caverns and small cut shafts, sliding downward and deeper into the rock. The car swayed as the track leapt over a chasm, infinite darkness extending above and below them. It looked to Andrew like the track abruptly ended a few yards ahead, but he felt no impending dread.

It was just the end of the running lights. They moved on along a darkened track, the line of yellow beams disappearing behind them. The lights inside the lift car were enough to dimly illuminate the rock walls as they slowed and entered another shaft. Andrew readied the security rifle, pushing the fixed stock into his shoulder and flipping off the safety.

"You remember where the safety is on that?" Andrew said, nodding to the shotgun.

Mariela nodded. She picked the gun back up and pointed to the little steel dot right behind the trigger. Andrew nodded back.

"Be careful. Don't shoot if you don't know what something is."

She nodded.

Mariela couldn't speak, and Andrew was content to let the lift move toward its final destination in silence. Slowly a light in the distance grew. The atmosphere outside began to whistle in the cracks of the car, which swayed slightly as it ran on. The growing light turned into an image – an open mining area, surrounded by the blackness of a natural cavern above, too high for the operating lights to touch. It was deserted, but a pale dust hung in the air, creating white halos around all the spotlights.

"There's been activity recently."

Mariela looked at him quizzically, as if she thought such a statement was obvious.

Finally, the car reached the landing and stopped. The track, which had run an unknown number of miles from the original mining colony, ended in a great steel stop covered with large rubber bumpers. The door opened.

Andrew stepped out quickly, checking the corners behind him and looking for any ledges above. When it was clear, he motioned for Mariela to exit, but he found she was already standing right beside him, holding the shotgun awkwardly, the stock clutched under her arm.

He nodded for her to follow him and continued visually checking every spot as he moved through the staging area. It was deserted and dusty. Computer terminals stood in the appropriate stations, but all the monitors were dim. A wide shaft ran downhill in front of them, lit by a long row of sodium bulbs. Due to the slope, Andrew could not see ahead.

He tapped a fist to his head. "Don't fail me now."

They started down the shaft, which he quickly realized was a full-width access tunnel, made for the passage of the heavy machinery which would be on the final and most active mining sector. He looked down at the floor and saw a litany of tracks in the dust, including those of a large steel-treaded digging machine. Each track was nearly three feet wide.

"How did they get something so big down here on such a rickety lift?" he whispered to himself. Mariela touched him to get his attention, then made a series of hand signs he did not understand. He jumped to the correct conclusion anyway. "They assembled them here. Makes sense."

Mariela nodded. She pointed ahead, and there the tunnel diverged into two. One set of tread tracks was new, the other old. Mariela pointed toward the new ones.

"Good thinking," Andrew whispered. "Of course, they could have moved anywhere." He heard something faintly, and he quickly pulled Mariela to the side and knelt down. "Did you hear that?" he said through his teeth.

Mariela shook her head.

Andrew strained. Faintly, he heard a voice, but he couldn't make out the words.

"This way. On your guard."

He moved down the shaft with the fresh tracks as silently as he could, hoping each time he heard a pebble bounce or scrape under the sole of his shoe that the people here were as dimwitted as the first ones he had come across. As he inclined his ear, he marked such chances as slim. The voice was repeating words, but he could not make them out. It was one voice. A man's voice, drowned in the reverberation of the long tunnel.

Andrew knew there was no real way to tell how far away it was. Underground, in tunnels and other spaces where sound could bounce around, distant noises could sound immediately close; things right next to you could sound incredibly far away. Everything would be distorted. But the voice was getting louder, and clearer.

Andrew stopped as he felt a pull on his arm. He turned to see Mariela cup her hand to her ear. She awkwardly put her shotgun in the crook of her elbow and gave Andrew a thumbs up.

Andrew pulled close, knowing that if he could hear the voice, even a whisper might carry back. He put his lips to Mariela's ear and said, "I can't make out what he's saying, can you?"

Mariela gave him an incredulous look and shook her head. She cupped her ear again and pointed to it, frowning.

Andrew shrugged and continued forward. The voice grew clearer. Finally, he made out one word clearly: *deeper*.

He stopped and whispered back in Mariela's ear, "Did you hear what he said?"

Once again, she gave him a confused look.

A few steps further in, through Andrew's focus and straining to understand, the voice suddenly became clear. He dropped to a knee and brought his rifle up, looking down the tunnel in anticipation.

Deeper. Down. Deeper down. Dig deeper. Deeper. Dig deeper down. Down and down.

Andrew's pulse quickened as the voice grew louder and clearer; the reverberation diminished. He waited for a vision of the future which would not come, silently cursing his decision to return to the deep.

Dig it deeper. Don't stop digging. Just a little further, and he'll be free. Free, you'll see. Dig deeper down.

The voice sounded like it was in his ear, but he could see nobody – nothing. Frantically, he looked to the ceiling, then behind him. Mariela stood holding her shotgun, watching the empty tunnel. The voice sounded like it was coming from her. She turned to look at him, and though her lips didn't move, Andrew was sure she was saying all the words.

Free him, be him, see him. Don't stop digging. Andy, Andy An-diggity-dig-down-dy.

Andrew could almost detect her lips moving, taunting him. He flipped off his safety, overcome with an urge to kill the demonic girl, the deceiver.

Deceivers, demons, oh yes, And-diggity-dy.

She had been playing him all along, pretending so that she could bring him down – deep down, where the digging was dug – and present him to the master, the demon inside. The *wrtla*.

And-diggity-demon-dy. Digging deep day by day. Oh yes.

Suddenly, the prescient side of his mind cried out in pain. He saw, burning into his sight, Mariela being dropped to the ground, beaten, shot. She was screaming and blood was splashing everywhere.

Andy – Andrew – realized he was the one doing it in the vision, and he snapped his head back and forth.

Kill her, Andy. Or let me do it. What do you want from her first?

Andy – that was himself, the other himself, talking. He saw Mariela backing away from him in the present, her shotgun leveled on him. He dropped his muzzle and held out a hand of surrender.

It was his past self. It had been talking the whole time, saying the same things over and over. With effort, he pushed it back. It had tricked him.

With a sickness in his stomach quite apart from the gun being pointed at his head, Andrew said, "I'm fine. Don't shoot me, please. I'm fine now. I was... tricked."

Mariela looked at him apprehensively. The muzzle of the shotgun was shaking with her unsteady forward left hand. She let the gun drop back down and she stifled a moaning cry. Though her face was contorted as if tears were coming, none came, for whatever reason. She sobbed softly.

Andrew stood up. *He's far more aware of what is going on than I thought. He waited for the perfect time to spring his trap for me – to take control.*

As his breathing slowed, he noticed another noise: the faint but unmistakable sound of grinding in the distance.

"They're digging," he whispered. "Digging down to free the *wrtla*. He's calling them... commanding them. We have to put a stop to it."

Mariela stared at him blankly.

Andrew looked up at the ceiling. "We can't kill them all. We'll have to... call in somebody else."

Mariela pointed at him.

Andrew nodded. "You're right. I'm what they called in. We're far out here, too. At least a few weeks travel from the closest Iber fleet base. We'll have to think of something."

He turned and moved on, closer to the sound of grinding stone – the sound of digging.

Eventually, the tunnel widened to a large, cavernous staging area, full of equipment and littered with tools. In the whole space, only two people could be seen. Seemingly genderless, they sat near each other in grey coveralls, holding an identical pose: their knees were pulled up against their chins, and they were almost imperceptibly mumbling, rocking slightly on their haunches.

Andrew hesitated. He could easily kill both of them before they could react, but he didn't bring a suppressor for his rifle. Of course, even if he had, the rest of the people in the mine would be alerted due to the echoing nature of the caverns. He slid out of the tunnel and over to a railed-in work area. A few of the computer terminals were on here, but clearly hadn't been touched in some time. A thick layer of dust covered everything and was caked onto the keyboards.

He watched his two marks carefully. He kneeled down to pause, then flinched as Mariela banged into a chair beside him. It hit the metal desktop and reverberated in the space. The two grey people did not move. Curious, Andrew began to move forward, then froze. He saw a vision of a few seconds in the future.

The two people were running toward them, screaming. In the vision, he felled both of them.

Strange, he thought. *Not my death, but theirs… unavoidable?*

He didn't have time to mull it over. Mariela bumped into the railing and it toppled over, all twenty feet of it. It apparently had never been secured to the platform. The heads of both people snapped toward them. They rose quickly, their eyes widening in alarm.

Andrew quickly shot each of them twice in the chest. The second victim – a woman, he could see now – staggered forward, unwilling to accept the reality that she was dead. Andrew shot her once again at center mass, and she fell like a sack of potatoes.

Andrew looked over to see Mariela shrinking against the desk, her gun forgotten on the ground. She had her ears covered.

"Damn," Andrew said. "I forgot you needed hearing protection. You'd better toughen up, I'm sure more of them are on the way." He tapped Mariela as he moved past her, over to another desk facing out on the platform, giving him some slight cover and a place to rest his rifle for better accuracy.

Nobody came.

Andrew allowed himself to listen to his past self – Andy – and heard nothing but the former ravings. Mariela had retrieved her shotgun. Andrew signaled her to wait. He hopped off the platform and went to a nearby pile of equipment. Amid the discarded elements was a pair of active earmuffs. They had been left on. Hoping the battery wasn't dead, he switched them off and then back on, relieved to see a small blue light let him know there was still charge remaining. He figured they had an auto-off feature.

He slung his rifle and went back to the platform. He helped Mariela down, who was very careful with her shotgun, then put the earmuffs on her head. He found the volume knob for the external microphone and cranked it up.

Andrew whispered, "You should be able to hear me really well now, but these will stop the guns from deafening you again, yeah?"

She nodded.

"Come on."

She followed him as he walked toward the sound of machines. Two dead bodies lay in a state of suspended decomposition near a cart, both their heads turned into smashed craters. The blood was long dried. On a garden world, one with insects and a full microbiome, it would have been a far more gruesome sight. As it was, it was just one more image to file away.

They entered another tunnel. The sodium lights were lying on the floor in a long strip, dimmed by layers of grey dust. It was almost foggy inside, so packed was the air with the debris of crushed rock. Andrew flipped on his flashlight as they neared the end of the light strand. It barely cut through the dusty dark, igniting countless motes in a long beam flashing out to the abyss.

The light caught a blank face, and Andrew froze. His prescient self had not foreseen anything. It was too late to wonder about that. The face contorted in anger and rushed forward, a hoot echoing from its gaping mouth.

Andrew fired straight into the mouth and watched the body drop. He swung the light, looking for more. It crossed two more faces, who likewise turned to attack. He dropped both of them. He took a moment to tap his head.

"Come-on, you," he said. He looked to Mariela. "You okay?"

She nodded and tapped her earmuffs. Andrew wondered if she would be able to shoot if – when – the time came.

They continued on, hearing the working of the machines growing louder, filling the space with a droning, horrible sound. His electronic earplugs worked to silence it, but it only increased his anxiety. Soon all he could hear was his own heartbeat and ragged breath. If he stopped and held it, he could hear, just on the edge of reality, Andy in his permanent prison, begging to come out and greet the *Wrtla*.

They came to a fork, of sorts. The greater part of the tunnel continued curving downward, but a small cavern was open to the side. There was some sort of refuse in front of the cavern – what looked like piles of dirty clothes. As they got closer, the light caught a pair of eyes. A slightly thin face lifted itself up from the pile. Its skin was taught and white, and it stared at the pair of them. Andrew did not hesitate. He watched the brain fly out the back and into the abyss behind it.

The refuse was, Andrew realized with horror, the remains of humans: empty, bloody clothes and piles of bones. He reached a hand back to signal Mariela to stay put. He turned as she screamed, only to have a future vision. He was seeing double – the future Mariela, and the present girl. The future one, stepping back in slow motion, was firing into an advancing man, ripping his flesh apart with three close-range blasts of buckshot.

The man, though, was cognizant in his face, pleading. His hands were up in surrender, not attack.

"Mariela get back! Get behind me!"

She was still screaming. Andrew pulled her by the back of her shirt. She nearly turned her gun on him, but froze as she saw his face.

He could still see the future. The man's face was open in both surprise and relief.

Andrew pulled Mariela behind him, and the vision disappeared. He raised his rifle, pointing his light beam where he had just seen the man. He could not help but see what Mariela had in the white reflected light. Just inside the entrance to the side cavern, there were human figures. Two of them were huddled over a body, squatting like some ancient savanna tribesmen, though not in the peace of such ancestry; they were dining, ripping flesh of sanguine hues bordering on black.

Andrew held still watching them. He didn't care about the future vision, or if either of these "humans" were capable of independent thought. He shot the closest one in the back of the head. Two clean shots tapped in and sprayed black gore on the further one. The remaining one didn't react for a moment, then realized that its companion was slumping over. It looked at the dead body curiously, then up at Andrew's light.

Andrew ended its existence with a slight pleasure that brought *Andy* forward hooting, only to be pushed back down.

"They're deaf," Andrew said, realizing the delay with each of his enemies in the tunnel. "Somehow they've gone deaf." He realized Mariela was gripping his arm with her free hand. He could feel her panting breath, though he couldn't hear it over the eternal thrud of the machines in the tunnel beyond. "Anyone would go deaf here, if subjected to it long enough and without protection. All they hear now is *It.*"

Andrew jumped and raised his rifle again as he detected movement down the tunnel. He held his fire and swung his light around to see the man from the future vision – or at least the one he thought might be from the vision. The details always became hazy and indistinct once he altered his actions.

The man was wearing a dingy and slightly torn white shirt, a half-buttoned orange work vest, and heavy duck trousers. He still had his shoes on, but they were untied. He walked stiffly, his arms flailing occasionally as if they had their own mind. His face was twitching, and every few steps he half-turned, as if desiring to run. His eyes, though, were fixed on Andrew's light. He started convulsing as he got closer, as if he were fighting some invisible attacker right in front of him.

"Stop!" Andrew shouted.

The man seemed to notice the word, but did not stop until he was a few yards from Andrew. Then he collapsed to his knees and gasped. His mouth was moving, but Andrew couldn't make out the words.

Carefully, he crept closer, his fingers twitching on his lips as if trying to pry them open.

"Please!" he said, his dry voice barely audible. "Please!" His hands went to his cheeks, and trembled there against the skin, as if wanting to dig into his flesh. "Kill me. Kill us!"

Andrew hesitated, wanting immediately to give in to the man's demand.

"Who are you?" he said, taking a step closer. He answered his own question as he saw the crooked name tag still on his vest. It was Ralph Esquivel, the plant manager.

The man didn't seem able to answer, but his eyes were desperate. He wore earplugs like Andrew's, though they were caked with black filth and long drained of power.

"I can't!" he said. "He made me! Now they'll dig him up and his voice will be everywhere! Kill us. Or he'll eat you too!"

"The children!" Andrew shouted. At the top of his voice he screamed, "Where are the children?!"

The man shook his head, his terrified eyes unable to break from their lock with Andrew. He choked and sputtered, then closed his eyes. "They can't work…" He looked to his left, into the cavern. His fingers were at his eyes, pushing into them, trying to reach behind the eyelids. "He made us eat. Can't starve. Can't leave. 'Til he's… He made us!"

Andrew gave into temptation and stepped to his right, to where the side cave opened up. He pointed his light inside. He hadn't really looked before. Now, he couldn't tear his eyes away.

He was vaguely aware, looking at the scene, that he ought to be feeling nausea, but his consciousness had become suddenly too detached to feel human. Or, perhaps, such reactions were part of Andy, and that one had been too tainted to find anything but perverse pleasure or humor in what was inside.

He was thankful, at least, that none of the bodies inside – small, once joyful bodies – were still recognizable as human. Their eyes were gone – devoured, perhaps, or destroyed as the mockeries of life they were. Time and the evil of the p;d *wrtla* he had known had saved a shred of Andrew's sanity, a sanity those empty eye sockets threatened to shatter. Andrew breathed, and his past self refused to show him anything of the victims. The seer of the past begged him not to look, but memories of the school flashed by his consciousness anyway.

The blast of Mariela's shotgun brought him back to the present, and Andrew spun around to see that she had shot the plant manager. He was twitching on the ground, blood flowing freely from many wounds to his chest. The girl's face was no longer horror-struck. It was iron-hard. She was holding her gun confidently, the stock pushed hard into her shoulder and her left hand steady, as if she had gained through the shock some return of control on that side of her body.

She stepped closer to the broken man. He looked up at her, his face almost relieved. He nodded slightly. She fired again, and his face disappeared in a spray of dark blood and bright bone that soon turned incarnadine in the beam of the flashlight.

"You shouldn't have looked."

Mariela glared at him, and he could read her face like she had spoken aloud, *He deserved to die.*

"No," Andrew said. "No, he deserved hell. What you gave him was a mercy, truly. He is free." He knelt down and glanced into the darkness, where he knew lay a satanic butchery that threatened his sanity. "My mark is dead, surely, but we can't leave yet. We can't let them release the *wrtla.*"

He looked at Mariela, who gave him a hard, appraising stare.

"I shouldn't have let you come," he said, "but you're here. We'll have to shut down their digging. Any idea how?"

Mariela shook her head. Andrew nodded and stood up, walking straight-backed toward the infinite noise at the end of the tunnel, no longer afraid of being heard. Mariela matched his pace. The tunnel went down and down, along an uneven and crooked path. All sound besides the digging and the internal sounds of his body disappeared. Time crawled by in the swinging beams of the flashlights. Eventually, they reached a cluster of large lamps enflaming a great cloud of dust.

Silhouettes of human figures were moving around the lights, which Andrew saw were attached to a great piece of machinery. It was like a tank, or armored vehicle, but larger, sitting on brown treads twice as tall as a man. The front of the machine was turning in circles, some diamond-faced set of tools grinding endlessly the stone in front of it, whittling it down slow centimeters at a time. A narrow drill bit sat poised above it, meant for longer excavations, not large tunnels. He didn't know how many people it took to operate as he could not see anyone in any kind of driver's seat.

The cluster of people around it were working endlessly on what the machine produced: millions of pebbles and piles of dust. The pebbles they threw by hand into nearby carts, automated to run along a magnetic track on the edge of the tunnel. The dust was pushed hastily to the side, kicking large amounts up into the air.

"Cover your mouth," Andrew said, flipping a switch to bring his helmet back around his face. The infinite sound immediately died down. "There are heavy metals in this dust." He saw that Mariela had wrapped her shirt around her nose and face. It would have to do.

Andrew didn't bother waiting. He took a knee.

"Watch our back!"

He began firing, holding himself in tight control. He dropped two silhouettes, and the others around it froze, then began moving toward him. He purposefully slowed his breathing as he felt Andy begging to gain control. He shot three more people. The lights began to get hazy in the background, and they were so bright his own flashlight was of little use.

Four more dropped. Two were crawling still toward him. He'd have to get them in a second. How many were coming now? Ten? Twenty?

He exterminated five more in five shots. He began to shake, and Andy began to laugh inside. Through his old self, he could hear the whisper of the *wrtla*. How close were they? Ten yards now?

He toggled over to auto, and fired, meaning to spray the group in front of him, but only a three-shot burst came out.

"Damn," he said, cursing his carelessness in not inspecting the autosear. He dropped three more. He was empty. Quickly, he exchanged his magazine for a fresh one.

His future self asserted some measure of control, and he saw a dozen forms spreading out around him. It only further confused him. Trying his best to focus, he continued to fire. He saw the shadows moving toward their slow-motion echoes, the places where they would be momentarily. With a quick appraisal, he fired as each one arrived, dropping six people, their blood blotting out the light behind them as they fell.

Again, he fired. He was losing track of where they were. Andy was yelling with mad glee, pushing into the center of his consciousness.

Empty.

He dropped out the magazine and reached for another. He fumbled it and dropped it on the ground. A field of future images flew out, immediately in front of him. Their hands, sickly white, were groping him, touching him in a tingle of future dread.

Andrew dropped the rifle and reached for his plasma gun. In the silence, he realized that Mariela was firing. He saw bodies drop to his left, but the images in front of him remained. He flipped off the safety and fired through the images. The muzzle flash of the energy weapon was powerfully bright in the dim tunnel, but the way it lit up all the dust around him was possibly worse. He was nearly blind, but he stayed focused on the images. The images disappeared as he hit the attackers which he could not yet see.

Finally, the last motion was a shambling corpse of a man heading toward Mariela. Andrew saw she was kneeling down, trying to reload the shotgun. He quickly dispatched the wretch, then moved to help her. Her shaking hands were having trouble loading the shells into the magazine tube.

"Next time use your pistol."

Andrew reached into her bag and grabbed a handful of shells. Taking the gun, he quickly popped them in, then threw one in the chamber and released the bolt. He picked his rifle back up and swung the light into the darkness behind them and saw motion that he couldn't clearly find the origin of out in the dust.

"The wrtla told them we were here," Andrew said, hearing laughter from Andy. "Stay close to me. Fire on them if you have to."

She obeyed, watching the space behind them that was flooded with the digging machine's lights. Andrew approached cautiously, watching his periphery as much as he could. Once he was fully in the halo of lights it was impossible to see any moving shadows. He tapped his head, hoping his prescience would alert him to any remaining enemies.

The machine seemed more massive as he approached, like a gigantic armored beetle with its head stuck in the sand. He slung his rifle and climbed up a ladder onto an operating platform that contained several seats. Each one, he saw, was controlled by a computer terminal and operation surface; manual controls were apparently locked. He touched one panel to bring it to life and it prompted him for identification and a password.

"Damnit," he said. He moved to the other three. All of them were identity locked. He began looking about frantically for an emergency kill switch. He shouted down to Mariela, "Do you see any switches? Anything to turn this thing off?"

On the ground, she turned from staring out into the darkness beyond the lights. She pointed at something on the ground level, between the treads.

Andrew quickly hopped down, falling to his hands as he hit the uneven pebble-strewn floor of the dig site. He found the switch, a large red button behind a plate of glass. He slammed the butt of his stock into the glass, shattering it, then something inside him snapped.

With horror, he realized he could hear laughing – *it was Andy*. He reached toward the switch, and his hand froze. He willed it forward, but it would not obey him. Slowly, his hand turned back, the fingers curling, as if the hand had a mind of its own and was struggling to make a fist. He could almost see a grimace there, in the lines of his palm.

Welcome back, child of darkness.

"I don't know you," Andrew said.

You know my sister, and therefore you know me.

"No."

Yes, Andrew Dalatent. Space is a small matter for us, distance irrelevant. Time belongs to us. We are inevitable.

"No."

You think we made a mistake with you? No, we did not. We do not make weapons idly. It is time for us to begin our great crusade, Andrew. The great work you were created for. All that you desire will be given to you; we reward those who are strong.

"I am free from you!"

Laughter answered him, but he couldn't be sure if it was the *wrtla*, or himself.

The next moment he was turning, facing Mariela.

She stood hesitantly, her eyes looking out across the dusty lightscape. Andrew felt a sudden heat in his neck, and he recognized an emotion that he had long been detached from – a consequence of his condition. *Emotion* was not the right word, he realized. It was a feeling, and it would have sickened him, but he was no longer in control. He was watching now, passively, and he realized that detachment from his past self no longer prevented him from feeling Andy's desires and compulsions.

Worse, he *was* Andy.

He considered for a long moment the lustful feelings that welled in him. There was simple, human lust, and a deeper, uglier feeling. A bloodlust. A lust for pain.

Kill her. There will be others. The demon tickled his mind with a promise.

He fired two shots into her chest. She crumpled into a heap. Her eyes looked up to regard him, sickening surprise filling the wide pupils as life left her body. Andy smiled. He had hated her from the moment he saw her.

Welcome back to the fold.

Andrew tried to resist, but he was failing badly. He felt gone, washed away and blended into oblivion. His fingers in his mind reached forward, trying to regain control and salvage something. He was a murderer, truly, now, but that didn't mean he had to let the *wrtla* win. Mariela's dead face recused him.

Something snapped, and Andrew realized he had lost time.

He was, he saw now, surrounded by the simple servants of the lord beneath. They waited on his whim, dominated by the thoughts of the being they had worked tirelessly to free. So many had died in their quest to please him, served him as food for the remaining slaves, who were hardened beyond any semblance of humanity now. They worked endlessly at his feet, pulling away the rubble from the great dig.

At last the digging machine broke through, its many bits and faceted tools worn down to round nubs by the effort. A black abyss opened beyond, and from it emerged the *wrtla* in all its terrible inverted glory. It was swirling gray smoke, seething and crawling out, covering every surface with millions of smooth, lacteous tentacles. Within that mist and mass of nocturnal opalescence squirmed pieces of its body – corporeal and yet beyond the physical realm, just as the mind of the lord was unfathomable and yet could be known and understood a piece at a time.

"Lord Dalrathag," Andrew said aloud, relishing in the name of his lord, knowable only once he had reached direct contact with him. Countless eyes of nothingness regarded him with pleasure, and Andrew leaned back, receiving the blessing of power from his god. Command and presence, to go with his foretelling and understanding.

Andrew – the Andrew who had withstood a *wrtla* and rescued himself, screamed internally at his impotence. His failure.

Darkness swirled. The prescient mind was sending a vision of the coming crusade, obeying the will of Andy and the *wrtla*.

Andrew was looking out from a window upon a scene of fire and carnage. A city was in ruins. Soon another lord would be freed. He laughed with pleasure. Gladness and satisfaction spread through his mind, tingling his body.

Andy laughed as the vision subsided.

He heard the voice of Dalrathag, omnipresent, soothing, "My servant, you shall be whole."

"As you will it," Andy said.

Pain, and then a fleeting wondering – do you remember pain in the space of nonexistence? Andrew realized the fractured psyche he had carefully formed was being folded in on itself.

Black nothingness enveloped his mind. Cold fingers twisted into fragile memories.

Then a little light appeared at the center and began to grow. It coalesced into form He was staring at a hand. His own ungloved hand.

He saw another hand move past his, and slam into a big red button. He turned his head to look upon the hard face of

Mariela. She looked at him, alarmed. The machine to his right began to quiet, the digging apparatus at the front grinding slowly to a stop.

He clenched his hand into a fist and turned around. Mariela had her back to him now, her shotgun held at the ready.

Shadows were coming in from beyond the halo of light. Sound was returning – footsteps echoed around them as the machine wound down.

"It was a vision," he said. He tried to focus, but inside he was screaming wordlessly against his past self, and he felt sick with the echoes of Andy's bloody lust. He reached in his pocket for the grenade he held there, to end things. He was too close to madness now. But then, Mariela was still alive.

A vision returned to him – he was alone in his ship. His fingers hesitated on the grenade. He cursed himself for not knowing which mind was sending it, past or future, or what he were trying to say.

A shadow turned into a person, running straight for Andrew, and Mariela fired. The attacker flopped forward, twitching. Another came in, and she fired again. She hit it somewhere on the side, but the faceless figure came on.

Andrew broke his paralysis. He took his hand out of his pocket and began firing. He put the closest one down quickly, then began firing into each moving shadow beyond the dusty lights. He didn't know how many he hit.

"We need to get moving," Andrew said. "We have to get out of here."

He strode forward. His prescience was not presenting him any information, perhaps tired from the exhaustive, years-long vision he had just lived. Andrew was too on edge to feel real fear about his blindness. He just knew he had to move forward.

As he got further away from the machine, his eyes adjusted, and he could see more people. They were milling about further up the tunnel, as if coordinating. He remembered the ones down here had minds that were more intact.

"Wait," he said, turning back. "They'll be able to start it again. Dalrathag will be able to command them."

Mariela gave him an incredulous look as he removed the grenade from his pocket.

"We have to disable it permanently." He adjusted the electronic fuse on the grenade so it would no longer explode instantly. He flipped the switch and threw it under the tread of the machine. "Run!"

He grabbed Mariela's elbow and pushed her forward, toward the swirling darkness and the figures beyond.

The grenade exploded, sooner than Andrew had intended. The blast threw both of them forward and covered them with a shower of small rocks and dust from above. Andrew helped Mariela up only to find a hand gripping the muzzle of his rifle, trying to twist it away.

Mariela fired on the attacker, knocking him away and showering both of them with a sudden deluge of blood. Andrew's visor was almost completely obscured by the gore. Desperately, he pressed the button at his neck to open it up.

They were surrounded by grimaced, dusty faces. Empty eyes.

Andrew panicked and shot wildly around himself. Mariela, he saw in his periphery, was retreating, her shotgun empty. He backed up toward her as he fired, desperately trying to aim with shaky hands and an overwhelming fear. He suddenly clicked empty.

"Mariela!" he shouted, running back and dropping the empty magazine. He fumbled a fresh one, but managed to get it in and release the bolt of the rifle. He turned again and fired at nothing he could see.

He was back at the machine. Mariela was nowhere to be seen. His heart fell as he looked upon the digging machine. His grenade had failed to do anything of significance. The heavy chassis was blackened, but the treads were intact.

He turned his head back at a cry from the hazy dark. He shouldered his rifle. His attackers were moving about, but his wild retaliation had stalled them. He heard the vocalization again, almost a scream.

A woman's scream.

"Mariela!"

He ran toward the scream, which was distinctly audible now that the machine had ceased its endless grinding. Through the settling dust, he could see figures moving; they were clearly as confused as he was in the bright, yet obscured, light, unable to hear his passing due to the deafness they endured.

A withered man reared up before Andrew's eyes. He barreled into the surprised thrall, checking him with the side of his rifle's receiver and sending him flying to the floor. The impact nearly knocked the wind from Andrew, but he scrambled on, trying to find the source of the scream. Just as suddenly, he saw the kneeling form of Mariela looking out into the darkness, her flashlight off.

Of course, they ignored her, they're looking for me, he thought.

He managed to stop and stoop beside her. Mariela, with a guttural note of fear, reached over and turned off Andrew's light. She then stood and guided him back along the wall, back away from the lights. Andrew looked back and as his eyes adjusted he could see more clearly the slaves of the *wrtla* moving together, fanning out into a net. They vocalized softly, wordlessly, like some imitation, or mockery, of babies. It was unlikely they could hear each other, but in the silence, the growing line of coos and grunts sounded like the song of insanity – the *wrtla* singing through grim, grey lips while it moved its toys about.

"You're right," Andrew said. "They can't hear us, but they can see us. This way, along the wall."

Andrew turned with Mariela and they felt their way up the tunnel, pushing themselves against the rough stone each time they heard the footsteps of one of the damned running past them, heeding the call of the master below. This happened with decreasing regularity, but no matter how long between the sounds, he and Mariela went as quietly as possible, just so that they could hear them. Andrew wondered if there were people down in the dark who could still hear. He did his best to still his breathing and avoid speaking.

Some amount of time later (it was hard to judge either distance or time while blind, and Andrew dared not check his computer for the hour, lest they be revealed by its light) they came upon the second cavern. Andrew discovered it when his feet ran into something heavy, yet soft, and he knew it was a body. They paused there, and Andrew considered crossing to the other side, blindly, or stepping through the bodies. He heard Mariela tap him and vocalize a wordless question behind him.

"We're at the cavern where the children... where we found the plant manager. We're going to have to cross blind here. Hold my hand." Andrew slung his rifle and took out his plasma gun. He reached back to feel Mariela's hand, then began to cross, shuffling slowly. He reached another body and, not knowing how to go back, tried to step over it.

He misjudged the distance and stepped on the far side of its ribcage. The body was significantly butchered and decomposed, and the ribs snapped under his weight, sending his boot down onto a bone, which rolled under him. He slipped and put a hand under himself. Ungloved, it ripped through some soft sinew and entered a cavity. The stench of rotting meat assailed him, and he didn't bother trying to stop himself from vomiting his meager stomach contents.

Even while he threw up, he pushed himself erect. He wiped his hand on his suit, then reached back for Mariela, who had let go of him.

"Find my hand." He snapped a few times, then felt relief as her hand closed on his, slightly resistant to the wetness. "I'm sorry."

Andrew helped Mariela over the body, and then they shuffled into a pile of bones. Not caring about the noise, they pushed through into empty, rough stone floor. After what felt like a long time scraping their feet along the floor, they reached the other wall.

"I think it's this way," Andrew said, pulling Mariela to his left. "At least it feels like it's going up." He chewed his cheek, hoping that he had not lost his bearings in the fall and wasn't taking Mariela back toward the digging machine and the waiting creatures.

The blackness stretched on. They passed noises of varying kinds: footsteps, vocalizing, talking with words, speech in a language neither of them recognized, snorting and snoring, and finally, the worst of all, the wet and sickening sounds of dining. All of them they passed by, and Andrew began to feel optimistic despite the horror of it all.

Then he heard, far below, the sound of the digging machine. Somebody among the hell thrall of the *wrtla* had enough capacity to start it back up. Dalrathag had purpose; he did not impose madness for its own sake, it seemed.

They tried to continue on, but without the sound to warn them, they grew tense. Mariela gripped Andrew's hand with increasing strength, to the point where he thought, had he a light, he would see marks in his flesh from her fingers and nails.

"They'll be heading backward to find us," he said. "We have to run for it." His heart leapt as he said this, his body finally responding to the brooding, sickening fear he had felt for so long in the dark.

Mariela paused, then squeezed Andrew's hand. She released him and flipped on her flashlight. Andrew did the same for the built-in light on his plasma gun. They looked around. They were somewhere in the tunnel, but they had no idea how far. They were indeed heading up, and that made Andrew feel relieved. He checked his computer on his wrist.

"I can pick up the wireless network signal from here. We'll definitely get back soon."

Mariela nodded.

They broke into a run. The incline was steeper than it seemed, and soon both of them were panting for breath. Andrew's suit felt stifling. He could feel a stream of sweat running down the back of his neck and pooling against his undershirt. They encountered nothing until they reached the point where the tunnels converged.

There, as their tunnel met the others, where the sodium lights remained in their eternal orange vigil, was a mass of people spread out into a long, tight line blocking the way forward.

They were men and women, all hunched and drawn thin. They weren't emaciated, but rather wretched – beings of deformed skin and musculature, made to function brutally rather than with beauty. The women seemed to lose their femininity, their sex determined as much by their old dress as any other feature. Their mouths were overlarge and darkened from their vile meals of flesh, and gaped as Andrew and Mariela approached.

Andrew did not wait for a battle plan; He strode toward the line and fired a bright white shot of plasma into the closest creature. It twisted away, its flesh burned and ripped apart by the energy of the blast. Andrew fired again, and again, but the creatures maintained some semblance of discipline. The *wrtla* was being liberal with his pawns, but he was still executing a strategy.

Andrew regretted throwing away the grenade when he did as the line of wicked moaning creatures became a semicircle hemming them in.

Mariela joined him, firing in the same direction. The line was close enough for the buckshot to do its magic, ripping soft flesh and maiming, even killing. She stayed to Andrew's side as they counter-advanced. When a man fell, the space was immediately filled, leaving a pile of dead bodies between Andrew and Mariela and the freedom beyond.

Andrew's plasma gun clicked empty, and he dropped the battery out and replaced it, then continued the carnage. An idea struck him.

"Cover your eyes!" he shouted as he put his arm across his own face. He used an old flaw of his plasma gun – he flipped the safety halfway on, which only slightly impeded the venting of the raw, hot matter from the gun. He pointed the gun up and forced the trigger down. It fired a shot of burning hot nitrogen in a cone above him, a burst far brighter than a single projectile burning through air.

Andrew uncovered his eyes and saw the thrall were recoiling in blindness. He pointed his gun to fire, but found that the shot had destroyed the breech. He threw the weapon hard to his right, where it hit a stooped woman. The thrall began to move toward her.

"Now!" Andrew said, bringing his rifle back around. He charged the line, waiting to fire until he was close enough to see the blind hollow eyes of his enemy. Rapidly, he killed three people. Mariela joined him, gunning down two that stood behind. Before they could fall, Andrew charged into them, knocking them down and bursting through the line.

Mariela screamed and Andrew turned back. One of the dying slaves had caught her ankle, as if suddenly realizing her existence. In their blindness, she was suddenly a thing to be noticed through touch. She had dropped her shotgun and was trying to draw the pistol tucked in her waistband. He stepped over a body and fired three times, killing the monster, but it had served its master well. Two more men gripped her legs. Andrew went to fire again, and found the rifle empty. He quickly checked his bag. He was out of ammo.

He hurled the useless weapon forward, striking one of the blind men, then he picked up the shotgun and fired the last three shots. Mariela at the same time fired into the closest man, emptying her magazine. Blood blackened by the artificial light poured in torrents, baptizing Mariela in sanguine horror. One thrall, unwilling to die, clung to her leg still, despite having most of its face ripped away by the pistol. A single blind eye stared up into the abyss from the part that remained. Andrew stepped forward and kicked the eye, breaking what remained of the skull. The thing twitched, but clung on in a kind of rigor mortis.

Andrew bent down and wrenched Mariela free, dragging her to her feet. She limped along beside him, running full out now from the hellthrall that followed behind, blind and dumb, but guided by a will that at the least could sense part of Andrew's mind.

As they ran, they could hear others joining the chase from some other corridor. They looked back to see eyes that had vision, and steps that had purpose. Even the blind were running wild now, guided by the intelligence below, which saw through the failing eyes of his puppets.

Finally, they reached the landing where the lifts were. By some grace beyond Andrew's understanding, the area was vacant. The *wrtla* had neglected to guard the final retreat, or else had deemed it unnecessary for his purposes. The lift car stood open, a white light in the eternal darkness, a fragment of color in unending umber-tinted horror.

"You get it moving," Andrew panted as they flew into the car. He quickly picked up his regular rifle and began firing at the approaching mob. It almost didn't matter now, nothing would stop them, but Andrew fired on. He emptied the magazine and threw a fresh one in. He toggled over to full auto and sprayed the ugly faces as they grew close, close enough Andrew could almost smell their rotting breath. He went empty again and reloaded.

Then the lift door closed. Andrew fired a single shot into the door. The tempered sapphire glass cracked as it caught the bullet, but did not shatter. A group of thrall slammed into the doors, rocking the car, but it was already moving. They slid off as the lift car moved into the dark tunnel. The monsters were leaping off the landing, scrambling through the tunnel in a mad attempt to catch them. Then the car slid over the abyss, rocking slightly as it ground along the track.

In the dim light, they watched bodies spill over into nothingness. Then the car went around a bend in the stone, and over a chasm.

They were alone in the dark once more.

"Take us straight to the main complex," Andrew said, leaning against the side of the car. "Don't stop anywhere on the way."

Mariela pointed to Andrew's gun, then held up four fingers.

"Not worth it. I have a few rounds left. There's bound to be a security station in the main compound anyway." He took a breath and looked at his hands. He wiped the sweat from his brow with the outside of his suit, which did little. Suddenly, the sweat felt cold. "I think the further away they get, the less they can understand. It's why your... the ones... in sector five, were so far gone. Who knows how many people are left, but I know nobody in the main area bothered to attack me, if anyone remained."

Mariela shook her head. She retrieved her notebook. *There's nobody left there. I checked.*

"Good. We'll be safe. Hopefully, I'll be able to disable the atmospheric generators." He caught Mariela's eye. "No, it's unlikely they'll use up all the oxygen, but we have to do something. We can't let them free the *wrtla*."

She nodded and wrote, *Better than nothing.*

They approached the sector four landing. A cluster of people stood on the landing, in the space where the cars passed, and on the rail above. The car didn't slow as it slammed into the crowd. Andrew brought his sights up and watched as bodies rolled over the windows, knocked down by the lift's running mechanism above. One of the thrall landed on top of the car. It swayed as it left the landing and moved back out into the dark. Andrew could just see the person above, struggling to move around and gain entry to the car.

Mariela was standing beside him; her pistol had apparently been abandoned and forgotten. Slowly, the person, withered and hollow-eyed, reached down toward the seam in the door. The glass was bulletproof; waiting for him to penetrate the doors to fire was agonizing. The monster lost some sense of footing and slipped down, falling away from the car into darkness.

Andrew relaxed and lowered his rifle.

They were out over the biggest abyss now, the running lights on the track the only way to tell they were going uphill. Suddenly, they saw the lights further up going black, one at a time.

"What?" Andrew said, squinting. His question was answered a few moments later when the other lift car came rushing by.

Mariela looked at him with alarm.

"It makes sense. They can use the digger, so of course they can use the lift." As if sensing her next question, he said, "The *wrtla* wanted full control of his slaves more than anything. If he let them go back up for food, he could lose them." He absent-mindedly touched his fist to his head. "So they ate..." Andrew shook his head, the images below returning to him briefly. "He must consider himself close to free. We're on a timer now."

The car went on in darkness, passing through the third sector landing and on into another stretch of blackness.

"We'll have to skip the atmosphere generators," he said. "No time, no point. Let's just live, eh?" He forced a weak and unfamiliar smile.

Mariela touched her chin in thought. She got out her notebook and wrote slowly *decompression?*

"We'd have to decompress all seven levels of the colony."

Mariela held up her finger as she flipped her notebook over. She drew something Andrew didn't recognize: a series of two-dimensional boxes lined up against each other.

"I don't know."

Mariela gritted her teeth, then wrote, *Heat.*

"The heat sinks. For the power plant. They wouldn't vent into the primitive atmosphere. Too thin. No point for that."

Mariela wrote *Top Level. Vents at TOP LEVEL. Emergency.*

"So punch a hole in the top of the power plant?"

Mariela nodded.

"Would that do much? It would take weeks to vent out the mine."

Mariela threw her hands down in frustration.

"Well, it's better than nothing, I admit."

Mariela began working the computer panel. Andrew leaned over and saw that she was punching in sector one as a destination.

"We don't have time," Andrew said. Mariela looked at him, impassively.

She picked her notebook back up and wrote *Explosives.*

They soon reached the landing for sector one, which looked out across a great underground canyon. In the distance the lights of the lower levels of the colony could just be seen, burning ever on despite the lack of anyone to see them. Mariela moved out of the lift car, limping slightly but going as close to a jog as her body and her nervous system would allow.

The second sector had at some point been converted to additional storage. There was nothing left to conveniently mine so high up, so the empty tunnels had been sealed by steel barricades which were now caked with dust. Mariela seemed to know the main area, and she quickly found a storage room with a locked door. She pointed at the doorknob.

Andrew sighed. He had discarded his plasma gun.

"Step back and cover your eyes." Mariela nodded and complied. Andrew took several steps back and shot at the lock. The bullet fractured and ricocheted, but the lock endured. He shot it three more times. The last time the mechanism within seemed to break apart, falling from the handle and clanging dully on the dusty floor.

Andrew tried the handle and found it stuck. With a grunt, he kicked hard at the door. It gave way and swung inward to reveal a room stocked with various types of explosives. She pointed at a case. Andrew nodded and picked it up, finding the small box heavy for its size. She grabbed a few other oddities that Andrew didn't recognize – blasting caps and ignition wires, he thought. She nodded and they quickly left the room.

When they got back in the lift Mariela quickly entered the coordinates for the main colony, and the lift car lurched out onto the floating track.

"We should have blown the track," Andrew said a few seconds later.

Mariela shook her head, as if that wouldn't have worked. "Why?"

She put down the equipment she held under her arm and wrote *Only work under compression. Dad did demo.*

Andrew thought back to a rudimentary engineer's course which dealt with demolition that he had taken when he was part of the Angl Space Force. The instructor had likened a firecracker going off in the palm of his hand – it would burn you, but you'd be fine, ultimately – with closing your hand around the same firecracker. You wouldn't have a hand after that.

"I should have used my grenade differently," Andrew said aloud. "I could have at least put it in the space between the treads and the driving gears. Haste makes waste, I guess."

Mariela looked at him blankly. Andrew made to answer the look, but her eyes grew wider and she stepped past him before he could begin the words. She looked out the rear window, placing her hands lightly on the window. Andrew shuffled next to her and looked into the blackness.

The other lift car was coming. It had just passed through the first sector landing. It seemed to be going slightly slower than their own car.

"Damnit," Andrew said. He released his magazine and checked it. He had nine rounds left. Quickly, he rummaged through his bag. He found two more stray cartridges and popped them into the top of the magazine, then put it back in the rifle. "Twelve shots, including the chamber," he said. "Just like the old west. Is there an emergency shutoff for the lift?"

Mariela nodded, but her face indicated a different emotion. She wrote, *Need a key.*

"Makes sense," Andrew said. "Any way to trigger an automatic shutoff?"

Mariela shrugged unknowingly.

"On the other hand, it would probably shut off the interior elevators as well." He sighed. The colony loomed closer. "Let's get there as quickly as possible. You know the way?"

Mariela nodded.

A minute or two passed in silence as the lift approached the final landing. At last, the lights grew close. The rock wall approached and the details of the windows looking out into the hollow mine could be discerned. The lift car slowed and finally arrived. The doors opened. Andrew and Mariela stepped out. The white light was almost nauseating after the darkness.

Andrew took a quick look around. He saw an access panel near the double doors of the mine lift and ripped it off. Inside were a number of breakers and fuses. He dropped the explosive case, put his gloves back on, and quickly ripped out what he could. Sparks flew and the power hissed. Several of the breakers wouldn't budge, so he stepped back and shot them a few times. The running lights on the magnetic track flickered and died.

"Nine rounds," he said aloud.

He looked out the window and, after a moment, saw the other lift car in the distance, a pin of light. It was still swaying, growing closer. As he watched, the first lift car pulled away, heading back into the mine.

"Shit," he said.

He glanced at the littered office around him and found a long screwdriver from a nearby workbench. He raced over to the doors and wedged it into the side of the second set near the wall. When he turned, he saw Mariela already limp-running to the main elevators. Andrew picked up the explosives and sprinted to catch up. She had already called one of the cars, and the doors were open. He followed Mariela inside and she punched in the top level.

"We don't have much time," Andrew said.

Mariela looked at him impassively. In the bright, incandescent light of the immaculately clean elevator, he could finally see clearly what they had endured. She was covered in blood, drying from crimson to brown, and her face was wet with sweat. She was trembling, too, on the edge of exhaustion. Andrew saw that his own hands were shaking and he was equally ugly with human death.

"How long has it been?" Andrew checked his wrist computer, unsure of the passage of time in the dark below. He tapped it, unbelieving.

Mariela was staring at him curiously.

"Almost three days? How are we still alive?"

Mariela pointed to her head.

Andrew wondered: did she mean her injury, or his?

The lift arrived at the first floor. Andrew followed Mariela away from the dormitories and schoolroom to another long, steel-lined hallway. At the end of it was a set of double doors that opened for them automatically. A reception area greeted them, empty and clean, with live computers but nobody to man them. Mariela paused for a moment, then went through a swinging door to an area full of terminals and basic workstations. She glanced around, then limped to another door. It opened into the power plant proper, a sleek self-contained set of rooms housing the fusion chamber, which plugged away its infinite hum without a care for the humans who had not attended to it. The door, apparently, had never been locked when the workers walked down into the mine... or had been carried away.

"There?" Andrew said, seeing the piping for the heat sinks leading from the free-standing central chamber up over a steel platform. Mariela nodded and limped on, carrying her equipment with her. They went up a narrow set of stairs to the piping, seeing the area where it divided. Half of the pipes went up, the others went another direction.

Mariela beckoned for the case. Andrew set it down and pried it open. Inside were stacks of tubes with elongated nozzles. Mariela pointed at him, then at the far door.

"I'll cover you," Andrew said. He turned and readied himself. In the bright, clean space it was hard to imagine the thrall from the mine. He could only think of human people. His past self gave him a fleeting vision of men and women at work in the room, pale translucent ghosts assembling the chamber at the center. Andrew refocused himself on the far door. He glanced back occasionally to check Mariela's progress.

Mariela slowly pushed the contents of the tubes into the space around the upper heat sink pipes. They vibrated slightly with the passage of coolant. As the thick, grey paste filled the area, she put in a narrow blasting cap, a simple electric-responsive explosive. She filled six of these narrow spaces, then quickly attached a wire to each blasting cap. Within a few moments, the paste had set. She ran the wires to a receiver.

Andrew saw her shaking so badly that she couldn't get the wire ends to fit into the terminals. He quickly kneeled down beside her and held the radio receiver. She guided each wire in carefully with her more proficient right hand. A sound from the other side of the room, distant and yet too close, made her wince.

"Just a few more, come on," Andrew said, not turning to look behind him. Mariela nodded and continued slowly inserting the wires, then closing the terminals.

Andrew, while he kneeled, was having a vision of the future. He saw six figures coming through the far door, right in a line. They were horrible to look upon in the clear, bright white light. They were dark... as if made of darkness, though somehow visible. Their skin was grey where it could be seen, but they were covered in filth, human waste, and the horror of their sustenance in the deeps. Andrew could see clearly the twistedness of them as they leapt over the railing and came bounding forward. Their mouths were slobbering open, too large for people, too small to be reptiles. Their eyes were over-large and dark. Their hair hung in strands, and their hands were like claws, or like the legs of some grotesque insect.

In the vision, he also heard. He heard their guttural cries, but he also heard the banging of the door. He knew that in the present, that sound had not happened.

"Stay calm, we'll be fine," he said. He watched the damned disperse, spread out to catch them in the future.

Mariela fidgeted, fitting the last wire into the detonation receiver.

Andrew heard the door slam open. Mariela put the receiver down. Andrew spun around and instantly saw three targets moving at a preternatural speed. He ignored the first two, who were already spreading out, and instead focused on the door. He fired once, and one of the thrall fell away.

"Eight."

The door opened again.

Andrew fired again. The shot didn't hit square. His vision shifted; he saw the fewer number trying to adapt, confused. The newly appeared thrall continued on, only injured. He fired again, this time hitting center mass. The figure collapsed on a ladder. In his vision, he saw a short one, what was once a woman.

"Six."

Andrew fired again, this time just as the door opened. The single shot hit a squat figure in the head, knocking it back.

"Five."

It stopped opening. One of the creatures that was already inside bolted for the exit; one sprinted directly at him and Mariela. Andrew focused on the bolting one, seeing a vision of him appearing from behind a steel workstation. He waited a few heartbeats, then fired as the beast revealed itself. The bullet hit, but it didn't kill.

The second one was on him; Andrew tore his eyes from the escaping monster and kicked out. His boot contacted the thrall, knocking it back, but it also latched onto Andrew's leg, taking him down with it. Andrew rolled, looking for a clear shot, but Mariela had already stepped over and was stomping on the thing, screaming at it.

It loosed its grip and Andrew rolled away. It grabbed Mariela instead, it was again as if it suddenly realized her existence; Andrew shot it once in the head. The skull came apart and the body stiffened. Mariela stepped back in disgust, then jumped over the body, beckoning Andrew onward.

"Wait," Andrew said. "There's more!"

He found it suddenly difficult to keep up with the limping, shuffling girl. He saw a phantom from the past and the future lining up over the door. As Mariela moved toward a staircase he kneeled down and fired. The door opened at the same time, and the creature was knocked back by the blast.

"Four," Andrew panted, getting to his feet and taking the steps two at a time behind Mariela. He grabbed her shoulder and stepped past her, kicking open the door. The hallway was empty, stained with a trail of blood. Two thrall were in their way, thrashing, fighting against death more than clinging to life.

Andrew froze for a moment, then put a shot in each of their heads, ending their fight. They had to climb over the bodies; it was impossible to step between them, and they seemed to give underfoot like something rotten.

"Two," Andrew said, dismayed.

He kicked open the door to the lobby. It was empty. He saw the trail of blood leading away, back toward the great lobby and lifts.

"Only way is forward," he said, stepping toward the exit. As they passed through the automatic doors, Andrew saw a flash of the future. It was confusing; he was alone in the landing zone.

Suddenly he turned around and saw a figure behind Mariela. The thrall was reaching for her. Andrew's finger twitched on the trigger, but he held it back with sudden realization. The creature was stepping around her, coming for him.

Not knowing what else to do, Andrew pushed Mariela into the wrtla-thrall with force. They both toppled to the floor. Andrew jumped over her and pulled the trigger.

The firing pin clicked, but the round didn't go off. Lacking the time to rack the bolt, Andrew stomped down with his foot on the creatures head. He vaguely thought he recognized the face – it was a woman's, but all his memory could tell him was that she was pretty, once. These thoughts circled hauntingly as he obliterated her twisted face, first with the heel of his boot, then with the stock of his rifle. He slammed it down over and over, until the skull split apart and the thing finally gave up its life to its master.

He breathed hard as he looked at it. It still twitched in spite of its exposed grey matter. It was wearing the remains of a dress. He racked his bolt and popped out the offending dud round.

"One," he said, helping Mariela up. She touched her chest as if in pain. "Sorry." Andrew pulled her along the blood trail toward the entrance. In the school lobby, he stopped. "We don't have an exosuit for you."

Mariela looked at him, dumbfounded.

"My ship is parked outside, not in the bay, since nobody was responding to hails. The atmosphere is too thin for you to breathe."

Mariela looked down at her right hand, which held the explosive remote. She put her shaky left hand on Andrew's shoulder, as if to resign herself to a goodbye.

"No," Andrew said. "I'll… Just come on."

She shook her head and pointed at the detonator.

"The ship is close to the airlock," Andrew said. "You'll survive. I know it. I can see the future."

She didn't give him an incredulous look so much as one that was disbelieving, but her face was also resigned, and yet somehow hopeful.

As they walked through the halls, the blood trail led on. Andrew looked at the once vibrant hallways, full of pictures and memories. False windows showing machine-made sunlight made shadows dance on the murals. How utterly devoid of meaning they seemed now, and yet his mind took them in. He took a last look at a child's drawing of a dragon, before focusing ahead. At last, they reached the front doors, the airlocks to the landing zone outside. The blood trail ended at the steel doors.

Mariela pointed down at the detonator.

"Now?"

She pressed a few buttons. Nothing happened for a long few moments. Mariela looked at the thing in anger, then they both felt a tremendous explosion through the ground. Smoke billowed into the distant foyer, and an alarm started sounding. Overhead, sprinklers began dripping.

Andrew linked his arm into Mariela's and led her to the airlock. It opened for him. He pressed a button and his helmet came back up. Most of the blood had dried into a smear fractured by the seams of the helmet's construction.

A vision assaulted him: it was one of the thrall. It was standing outside on the hazy planet surface, pointing a rifle at Andrew, firing it into his face. Vaguely he could see, as he fell, airlock doors.

"When it opens, run," he said as he pressed the button to open the other door. He shouldered his rifle with his free arm. The air rushed out, meeting the thin, almost red atmosphere.

Nothing was there. Andrew did not have time to puzzle over it. He pulled Mariela out.

It was sunset outside, which could last for many hours on the slowly rotating planet.

They dashed for Andrew's ship, Mariela holding her breath and limping as fast as she could. She started gasping. Then she fell. Andrew dropped his rifle and scooped her into his arms. As he approached the ship, the airlock doors opened for him, recognizing the unique signal on his computer.

He was struck with a future vision. He had seen it before. He was alone in the cockpit of his ship. Instinctively, he turned. He saw the bloody thrall right behind him, fazed by the thin atmosphere but far from dead. It was holding his rifle.

It pulled the trigger.

Nothing happened. Andrew chanced to tilt his head and saw – to his surprise – that at some point he had flipped the safety back on.

He backed up two steps as the thrall tried again to fire the weapon. The airlock doors closed. Finally, the thrall figured it out, and the last shot slammed into the door. Andrew hit the lock button with great force and turned away with Mariela in his arms, not bothering to watch the Thrall try to claw his way in with what remained of his driven, demon-powered stamina. The vision of himself alone persisted, and Andrew began to despair.

He brought Mariela into the main hold and laid her down on the floor. He found a weak pulse and quickly bent down to breathe into her, his helmet peeling away as he did so. He pressed his mouth against her cold, pale lips. He pushed hard and felt her collapsed lungs resist, then peel open slightly. He looked around; he had forgotten where he placed his medkit. He bent down again and pushed out another hard breath into her mouth. The lungs gave way again. He took a quick second breath and pushed with all his might.

She sputtered and coughed, wracking with the effort. He leaned back. Suddenly, he remembered where his medkit was. He returned a moment later with an oxygen tank and a mask, which he placed over her head. He opened the valves and allowed the gas to flow in. Her weak breaths continued.

Then her eyes flipped open. They crossed and moved erratically, then blinked and found him. She coughed and sputtered again.

"Breathe slowly. You tried to inhale the atmosphere and it collapsed your lungs." He smiled at her, then stood up. With a touch of his wrist computer, the engines started up. He went down to the airlock and checked the window. The thrall was lying on the ground, his rifle next to it. Far beyond the body, at the colony, there was a plume of white gas venting, kicking dust up into the atmosphere.

"You can keep it," he said, panged to leave his favorite tool behind, but too exhausted and afraid to open the door and retrieve it.

He sighed, then headed back up to the hold, where Mariela was sitting up, leaning against a padded bench.

"We still need to get off this rock," Andrew said. "The lifts..." He trailed off, meeting Mariela's gaze. Gently, he picked her up and put her on the bench. She leaned over, holding the oxygen mask close to her face, and curled into a slight fetal position.

Andrew watched her slow her breathing, then strode up to the cockpit and began the sequence for take-off. He was alone, he realized, and the vision of the future became memory, a thing of permanence.

He waited for his future self to alert him of anything, but it was silent. The part of his mind that could see the past was replaying memories of the colony, but those were too painful, too weird, for him to attend to. His former self, *Andy*, was strangely silent.

"Always alone," he said aloud, checking over all the systems on the computer readout.

With the engines on full, the ship lifted off. Andrew could see the venting plume better now. It was bigger than he expected, but he knew the vastness of the caverns would still take time to decompress. He hoped it would not be too long. He said a silent prayer, knowing the act would prod Andy, but not caring. He begged and gave thanks, his hands trembling on the ship's control sticks. The *wrtla* still beckoned, threatened, was raving to be released, but the prayer pushed him – and Andy – into a barred well of darkness. He looked up. He put a routine into the computer during the automated liftoff to put out a bulletin when they approached the next beacon to stay away from the planet.

He took over the ship's guidance and brought it slowly up to orbit, where he set the computer to work on the trajectory for the closest settled system. He breathed out heavily. As the ship moved out into space, readying itself for a rapid acceleration past light speed, he went back to the hold.

Mariela was laying on the bench, sleeping softly, the oxygen mask slightly askew. Blood was caked in her dark hair, and circles still hung under her shadowed eyelids. Andrew sat down cross-legged in front of her and leaned against the wall, watching her slowly breathe.

"Not so alone."

Andrew closed his eyes.

End.

ABOUT THE AUTHOR

David Van Dyke Stewart is an author, musician, YouTuber, and educator who currently lives in rural California with his wife and children. He spent the majority of his 20s as a musical performer and teacher in California and Nevada before turning his attention to an even older passion: writing fiction. He is the author of *Muramasa: Blood Drinker, Water of Awakening,* the *Needle Ash* series, and *Prophet of the Godseed,* as well as numerous novellas, essays, and short stories.

You can find his YouTube channel at http://www.youtube.com/rpmfidel where he creates content on music education, literary analysis, movie analysis, philosophy, and logic.

Sign up to his mailing list at http://dvspress.com/list for a free book and advance access to future projects. You can email any questions or concerns to stu@dvspress.com.

Be sure to check http://davidvstewart.com and http://dvspress.com for news and free samples of all his books.

Printed in Poland
by Amazon Fulfillment
Poland Sp. z o.o., Wrocław